MANDIE®
AND HER
MISSING KIN

Mandie® Mysteries

Mandie and Mollie: The Angel's Visit

MANDIE®
AND HER
MISSING KIN

Lois Gladys Leppard

BETHANY HOUSE PUBLISHERS
MINNEAPOLIS, MINNESOTA 55438

Mandie and Her Missing Kin
Copyright © 1995
Lois Gladys Leppard

MANDIE® is a registered trademark of
Lois Gladys Leppard

Library of Congress Catalog Card Number
95–42319

ISBN 1–55661–511–6

Cover illustration by Chris Wold Dyrud

Published by Bethany House Publishers
11400 Hampshire Avenue South
Bloomington, Minnesota 55438
www.bethanyhouse.com

Bethany House Publishers is a Division of
Baker Book House Company, Grand Rapids, Michigan.

Printed in the United States of America

This book is especially for all you people in and around Franklin, Macon County, North Carolina, and Swain, Jackson, Buncombe, and Transylvania counties.

My mother's people—with the names Wilson, Duvall, Buckner, Guyer, Roper, Downs, Frady, Bryson, Pittman, and many more—came from these counties back in Revolutionary War days, before the land was divided into the present counties.

My mother, Bessie Addiavenia Wilson Leppard, was born in a log cabin at Charley Gap on the present site of Nantahala Inn in Swain County. Her grandfather, Abel Buckner, who owned property and raised his own family at Rose Creek near Franklin, was the first white man to cross the Nantahala Mountain. He bought land from the Cherokee Indians in Swain County. He and his family were among the founders of Maple Springs Baptist Church, and my grandmother, Amanda Elizabeth Buckner Wilson, is buried there. Mandie in my books was named after her and patterned after my mother.

Uncle Ned in the Mandie books was my mother's grandfather, Ned Wilson, who was Cherokee. He lived to be 112 years old.

My grandmother Wilson was born at Rose Creek. Her father and mother, Abel Buckner and Rebecca Elizabeth Guyer, were married in 1815 in the Guyer home near Franklin, and the marriage was recorded in the old courthouse records.

Are we related? Kin or not, I love you all.

Lois Gladys Leppard

About the Author

LOIS GLADYS LEPPARD worked in Federal Intelligence for thirteen years in various countries around the world. She now makes her home in South Carolina.

The stories of her mother's childhood as an orphan in Western North Carolina are the basis for many of the incidents incorporated in this series.

Visit her Web site: *www.Mandie.com*

Contents

"But I say unto you, love your enemies,
bless them that curse you,
do good to them that hate you, and pray for
them which despitefully use you,
and persecute you"
(Proverbs 3:13–14).

Chapter 1 / Journey Into the Past

Mandie Shaw beamed with happiness as she told her grandmother goodbye on Mrs. Taft's front porch. She had been allowed a few days off from school to go home with Joe and Dr. Woodard.

"Thank you, Grandmother," Mandie said as she embraced Mrs. Taft with one arm and held on to Snowball, her cat, with the other.

"Now, Amanda, I am trusting you to be on good behavior while you're visiting the Woodards," Mrs. Taft reminded her as she put her arm around Mandie's shoulder. "I am doing this without your mother's knowledge, since it would take too long to let her know. So please don't make me sorry I did it."

"I won't," Mandie promised, then grinned up at the lady and added, "and I'll have to behave because Mrs. Woodard would never put up with me otherwise."

"Yes, I know how you usually manage to get

your way with other people," Joe teased as he stood on the steps.

Before Mandie could reply, Mrs. Taft called to Dr. Woodard, who was tightening the straps holding Mandie's valise in the back of his buggy. "Please let me know if Amanda lives up to her promise—and give my love to Julia."

"Oh, I will," Dr. Woodard said. He glanced over at Mrs. Taft and then smiled at Mandie. "But I'm sure she will be a perfect young lady. And I'll tell my Mrs. that you sent your regards."

Mandie ran down the steps to the waiting rig, and Joe gave her a hand up to the seat. He climbed in after her as Snowball settled in her lap.

"Do you think we'll have enough room on this seat for three people?" Mandie asked as Dr. Woodard sat down on the other side of her. She had ridden many times with Dr. Woodard and Joe in this same rig, but she was growing older now and was more aware of Joe's presence so close.

"Of course," Joe said with a laugh. "I don't believe any one of us has got any fatter."

"I hope not," Dr. Woodard said, a smile breaking the serious expression on his face. "Else we might just have to leave someone behind."

Mandie looked at him as he picked up the reins and said, "I could ride in the back."

"No, you can't. It's full of our baggage," Joe said with a satisfied grin.

Mandie shrugged and waved to her grandmother, who was still standing on the porch. Dr. Woodard shook the reins, and Mandie drew a sigh of relief as the horse pulled the buggy forward. She was going home with the Woodards! They had been her father's neighbors at Charley Gap when he was

living. And her grandmother had allowed this un-
scheduled time away from school because Mandie
had solved a mystery dear to Mrs. Taft's heart, and
because Miss Prudence had jumped to wrong con-
clusions regarding the matter.

Mandie was suddenly aware of Joe staring at her
as they traveled through the streets of Asheville,
North Carolina, and on out into the countryside.
She smiled at him.

"It won't make you any fatter to talk, you know,"
Joe teased.

"Joe!" Mandie exclaimed.

"I wonder what your grandmother put in the picnic basket she gave us," Joe said, acting serious.

"Why, I can tell you that," Dr. Woodard said as
he glanced at the two young people.

"What?" Mandie and Joe asked simultaneously.

"Your grandmother put *food* in that basket, of
course," Dr. Woodard said, looking straight ahead.

"Of course, but what *kind* of food?" Joe asked.

"The kind you eat," Mandie quickly told him.

Joe sighed and said, "All right, the riddle is
solved. But I do hope there's fried chicken in the
basket."

Mandie was thirteen years old and Joe was two
years older. The two had been lifetime friends and
Mandie knew how much Joe liked to eat, but she
was wishing he'd get his mind onto something else.
This was a serious journey for her, and she wanted
to think for a while about her father, who had died
the year before—about how happy she had been
when he was alive and how much she had loved
him. Her throat made a quivering sound as she took
a deep breath.

Joe immediately reached to hold her hand. "I

know what you're thinking about, Mandie," he said. "I'll be quiet awhile." His brown eyes looked into her blue ones.

Mandie squeezed his hand and cleared her throat without speaking. Then she smiled at him and asked, "Does my father's house really look abandoned?"

"The grass and weeds have grown up all around it, and I didn't see any livestock anywhere near there," Joe said. "I came down the hill by the house right before we came to Asheville, when I put flowers on your father's grave for you."

"I hope no one is living there anymore, so I can go in the house and look around," Mandie told him. "It's been way over a year since I left there."

"We'll find out what's going on," Joe replied. "And if the house is empty, we'll get inside somehow, even if it's locked."

"Locked?" Mandie asked as she realized this could be true.

"Locked," Joe repeated. "But you know, locked doors have never kept us out of other places we've explored."

Mandie smiled at him and said, "Right. We'll find a way."

———

The roads through the North Carolina mountains were rough, and travel was slow in 1901. At noon Dr. Woodard pulled the buggy up by a stream cascading down the mountainside, and Mandie and Joe opened the picnic basket Mrs. Taft had packed for them.

On top was a large tablecloth, which the two young people quickly spread over a grassy spot while Snowball meowed from the bush where Mandie had tied his red leash.

Joe began removing the food from the basket and exclaimed, "Aha! Fried chicken! And lots of it."

Mandie took out buttered biscuits wrapped in a large white napkin.

"And chocolate cake!" she exclaimed as she pulled out half of a three-layer chocolate cake that her grandmother had tucked in the end of the basket.

Dr. Woodard sat down on a tall rock nearby and said, "Will y'all hurry up with that food? Snowball and I are hungry." He laughed.

Mandie smiled and handed him a plate. "Help yourself," she said. "We've got it all unpacked."

Dr. Woodard stepped over to fill his plate and then sat back down on the rock. The two young people quickly loaded their plates and sat on the grass.

Snowball strained against his red leash and began fussing loudly when he smelled the chicken. Mandie smiled at him, pulled meat off a drumstick, and placed it in front of him. He ate as if he had been starved.

Mandie looked at Dr. Woodard and remarked, "I hope Mrs. Woodard won't mind my bringing Snowball to your house."

"One more animal won't make a bit of difference," the doctor said. "But you'll have to keep up with him and see that he doesn't run away."

"I will," Mandie promised between bites of chicken.

"And I'll probably have to help," Joe said with a groan. "I know how much that cat likes to disappear." He looked at Mandie and grinned.

"Just don't forget how much Snowball has helped us solved mysteries," Mandie reminded him. She reached back into the picnic basket and asked, "Now how about a hunk of this chocolate cake?"

Joe and his father each took a large slice. Mandie took a smaller piece and shared a bite with Snowball, who would eat anything his mistress ate.

As soon as they finished their meal, they took cups from the basket and filled them with water from the falls of the icy mountain stream.

"Drink your fill. We won't be stopping again until we get home," Dr. Woodard told the young people.

Mandie finished her drink of water and filled the cup again for Snowball. His nose twitched when it touched the cold water. He looked up at his mistress and then slurped it up.

After they had repacked the basket, they climbed back into the buggy and Dr. Woodard guided the horse over the mountain road.

In the late afternoon, Mandie became excited when she saw the Woodards' two-story log house come into view. She had visited there before, so she knew there were four large bedrooms upstairs, crammed full of huge beds with headboards that almost reached to the high ceiling. The Woodards enjoyed having company and had plenty of room to accommodate quite a few guests.

"Thank the Lord we made it safely home," Dr. Woodard said as he stopped the horse in front of the long veranda and stepped down from the buggy.

Mandie, holding on to Snowball, followed Joe. Dr. Woodard walked to the rear of the buggy and began removing the straps holding the luggage. Joe helped him as Mandie watched.

Suddenly Snowball hissed and stretched his claws into the shoulder of her dress. Mandie looked around and saw Joe's dog, Samantha, racing toward them. She was squealing with delight at having her master back home. Joe bent to pat her head. The beautiful golden brown dog whined with pleasure.

"Snowball, stop it," Mandie told her cat as he hissed at Samantha. She pulled his claws out of her dress and held his front feet so he couldn't put them back on her shoulder.

"Oh, Samantha, where are your babies?" Joe asked his dog as he looked around the yard.

"Samantha has some new babies?" Mandie asked as she glanced toward the house. "She had babies last year when I was here, remember?" She turned to look at Joe as Dr. Woodard pulled down her valise and set it on the ground.

"Yes, she did," Joe said, straightening up to grasp a large bag from the back of the buggy. "And she has more now. We gave the other ones away when she had the new ones."

"We didn't need so many dogs," Dr. Woodard remarked as he carried his bag and Mandie's valise up the front steps. Joe carried the other bag, and Mandie followed him.

Mrs. Woodard was standing in the front doorway. "Amanda, how nice to see you!" she said.

Mandie looked up and smiled as she approached the woman. "And it's nice to see you, Mrs. Woodard."

"My, my, that cat sure has grown," Mrs. Woodard remarked as she looked at Snowball.

"Yes, ma'am, he has," Mandie agreed, looking up at the lady with her blue eyes. "I hope you don't mind me bringing him with me." She pushed her bonnet back on its strings and smoothed stray tendrils of blond hair.

"Not at all, dear. But I suppose you'd better keep him inside the house. Samantha has puppies, you know, and she might not like him around them. Joe can make a sandbox for him," Mrs. Woodard said.

"Thank you," Mandie said.

Dr. Woodard set his bag down inside the doorway and turned back to embrace his wife and plant a quick kiss on her cheek. Mandie smiled to herself when she saw Mrs. Woodard become flustered with the show of affection. Mandie thought of her father and wished with all her heart she could see him and her mother do such a thing.

"Let's get Amanda settled now," Mrs. Woodard said, turning away from her husband. "Come on, Amanda, I'll take you upstairs," she added.

"You don't have to walk all the way upstairs, Mrs. Woodard, if you'll just tell me which room I can sleep in," Mandie said. She wanted to give Dr. Woodard a few minutes with his wife to catch up on what had happened during his trip through the mountains to visit patients before he finally ended up in Asheville.

"Well, dear, just put your things in the far room on the front, the one you used last time, and then hurry on back down. Supper is almost ready," Mrs. Woodard told her as they all stood in the front hallway.

"I'm coming, too," Joe said. He picked up his father's bag and said, "I'll take this upstairs."

"Don't be too long," Dr. Woodard said.

Carrying his own bag in one hand and his father's in the other, Joe made slow progress up the steps behind Mandie. She held Snowball with one arm as she brought up her bag.

"Meet you downstairs in two minutes," Mandie called to Joe as she turned down the corridor toward the room designated by Mrs. Woodard, and he went in the other direction.

"Right," Joe agreed. "If you want to just leave Snowball in your room, I'll run right out and make a sandbox."

Mandie turned around and said, "I forgot about that. I think I'd better stay with Snowball until you bring the sandbox."

"I'll hurry," Joe said as he continued down the hallway.

Mandie set Snowball down in her room and quickly unpacked the few things she had brought with her. Since she would only be here a few days, she didn't need much.

By the time she was done, Joe had come hurrying in with the sandbox. "I'll put it over here on the hearth so Snowball won't scratch the sand and throw it all over the rug," he said as he placed it to the right of the fireplace.

"That's a real good idea. Sometimes he gets all wound up scratching around in his sandbox," Mandie said with a little laugh as she watched her cat head straight for the box.

"We can bring him some food after we eat," Joe said. "Come on. Let's go downstairs. I'll run back up with a pan of water for him."

When the two got to the bottom of the stairs, they found Mrs. Woodard waiting for them with water for Snowball. "I expect your cat will be thirsty after that long journey," Mrs. Woodard said.

"Be right back," Joe said as he reached for the

container and ran back upstairs with the water.

Dr. Woodard came into the hallway from the parlor and asked, "Are we ready to eat now?"

"Yes, all ready," Mrs. Woodard said as Joe came bounding down the stairs.

When they went into the dining room, Mandie saw that Mrs. Miller, who lived with her husband in a cabin on the Woodards' property, was putting food on the table. The Millers were tenant farmers.

"Hello, Mrs. Miller," Mandie said, smiling at the woman.

"And hello to you, Miss Amanda," Mrs. Miller replied, as she placed a platter of food on the table.

When everyone had been seated, Mrs. Miller said, "I believe I have everything on the table, Mrs. Woodard. I'll be cleaning up in the kitchen if you need me."

"Thank you, Mrs. Miller," Mrs. Woodard replied as the woman left the room.

Mandie enjoyed the food and the conversation as Dr. Woodard discussed what had happened during various visits to patients, and then Mandie related the latest events that had taken place at her school.

When there was a pause in the conversation, Mandie was finally able to ask the question that had been on her mind ever since she had arrived at the Woodards'. "Mrs. Woodard, have you heard anything, or do you know anything, about . . . uh . . . whether or not those people . . . uh . . . or anybody . . . is living in my father's house?" she asked, stumbling over the question. She couldn't bring herself to call the people "kinpeople" who were supposed to be living in her father's log cabin.

Mrs. Woodard looked at her thoughtfully for a

moment, then replied, "No, can't say that I have. But then those people stay pretty much to themselves. They don't get out and around much, so other folks more or less leave them alone."

Joe spoke up. "It looked abandoned last time I saw it. The grass was all grown up and full of weeds, and there was no sign of anybody or anything around."

Dr. Woodard cleared his throat and explained to his wife, "That's the reason Miss Amanda came home with us. Mrs. Taft gave her permission to come and visit so she could go and see for herself whether anyone is living there now or not."

"Oh, indeed," Mrs. Woodard said, looking back at Mandie. "What will you do if the house is empty, dear?"

"I'd like to go inside. You see, I haven't been back since my father died and I was sent to work for the Brysons," Mandie explained.

"And Uncle Ned her father's old Cherokee friend, took her to her uncle John's house, if you remember," Dr. Woodard added.

"Yes, of course," Mrs. Woodard said.

"Do you think I could run over there as soon as we've finished supper?" Mandie asked as she looked from Mrs. Woodard to Dr. Woodard. "It'll be daylight for a while yet."

"I don't see why not," Dr. Woodard said. "Joe can go with you, but y'all must come straight back before it gets dark."

"Oh, thank you, Dr. Woodard," Mandie said.

"Take Samantha with y'all," Mrs. Woodard told Joe. "She needs the exercise. She stays right around the yard since the puppies came."

"Yes, ma'am," Joe agreed.

Shortly thereafter, Mandie and Joe set off down the road, with Samantha racing ahead. She would stop now and then and look back to be sure her master was following, and whenever Mandie and Joe almost caught up with her, she would take off again.

"Smart dog," Mandie remarked with a laugh, but her mind was on what she might find when they arrived at her father's property.

"Yes," Joe agreed as he glanced at Mandie.

No more was said until the rail fence that lined Jim Shaw's land came into view. Then Mandie stopped suddenly in her tracks and caught her breath. Her father had been putting up that fence when he died. She could see him in her mind—his curly red hair, bright blue eyes, and his constant smile. It seemed like only yesterday, but in fact it had been well over a year ago. And so much had happened since then.

Joe reached for her hand and squeezed it tightly. Mandie's blue eyes were full of tears as she looked up at him and said with a shaky voice, "I'm ready to go on."

They walked together hand in hand as they passed through the open gate and came to the barn.

"We'd better stop a minute and look ahead," Joe whispered to her.

Mandie nodded, and the two peeked around a corner of the barn.

"Oh, what a mess!" Mandie said as she glanced around the yard. Joe had been right. Weeds were growing everywhere. Trash was strewn here and there. The house looked deserted.

Mandie looked through the half-open door of the

barn. There weren't any animals inside and the place looked filthy.

"Let's walk up to the house and knock on the door," Mandie suggested in a whisper.

Joe looked at her and asked, "Are you sure we ought to do that? There may be someone in the house, and if they open the door, what are we supposed to do?"

"We'll just see who it is then," Mandie said. "Besides, I don't believe there's anyone around here. Come on."

Mandie moved along the wall of the barn to the corner. She paused and then cautiously walked forward into the open yard between the barn and the house. Joe followed. When she reached the door of the log cabin she paused again. Memories came through her mind, but she determinedly put these aside and knocked loudly on the door. She listened but couldn't hear a sound inside. She knocked again and again without receiving an answer. Joe waited behind her.

"There's nobody in there," he whispered.

"Let's go in," Mandie whispered back as she reached for the doorknob. She slowly turned it and pushed on the door, but nothing budged.

"Locked," Joe whispered from where he watched.

Mandie sighed loudly and stepped over to a window. She tried to look inside, but a curtain blocked her view. She walked all around the house, trying the back door and trying to see through the other windows, but without any luck.

"How can we get inside?" she asked. "There has got to be a way."

"It's too late tonight, Mandie," Joe told her. "We

can come back tomorrow."

Mandie glanced at the sky and realized the sun was going down. "I suppose we'll have to," she said with disappointment.

"We'll come back right after breakfast tomorrow," Joe promised.

"All right," Mandie said, taking a last look at the house as she walked slowly toward the road.

Joe looked around the yard and asked, "Now where did Samantha get to?"

"I don't know," Mandie said as she realized she had not seen Samantha since they had entered the yard.

Joe hurried on toward the road, watching for his dog. Once on the road, he began whistling for her. "Samantha!" he called.

Mandie was surprised when she saw the dog running toward them from the direction of Joe's house. "She must have gone back home," she said just as Samantha reached Joe.

"I suppose she had to go back to see about her puppies," Joe said as he stooped to rub Samantha's head. "Let's go home now, Samantha, home!" The dog turned and started back toward Joe's house.

Mandie stopped at the bend in the road for one last look at her father's house. Evidently no one was living there anymore. And tomorrow morning she and Joe would figure out some way to get inside. *What will we find?* she wondered. *Will it look like it did when I lived there with my father?*

And where had everyone gone? Why did they all go off and desert the house? Etta and Zack Hughes . . . Irene . . . when did they leave?

Mandie could not sleep much that night with all this on her mind.

Chapter 2 / Who's There?

The next morning after breakfast, Mandie and Joe once again set out to visit her father's property. Samantha followed for a while, but then turned and raced back toward Joe's house.

"Evidently she is going back to her puppies," Joe remarked as they walked along.

Mandie had been carrying Snowball because he had insisted on hissing at Samantha. Now that the dog was gone, she set her cat down to walk at the end of his red leash.

"Maybe Snowball will behave now," she said. Then laughing, she added, "It's too bad my cat and your dog can't get along together."

"That will never be," Joe said. "Remember how Snowball used to follow you to school when you lived here? And then Samantha would sometimes show up, and we had to keep them apart."

"I sure do," Mandie said with a smile. "Joe, let's

go by the schoolhouse. I haven't seen it since I moved away from here."

"All right," he agreed. "Mr. Tallant is still the teacher and everything's more or less the same."

They turned down the narrow road that led to the school building.

"I wish I could come back," Mandie said.

"That wouldn't be a good idea because you need more education than Mr. Tallant is capable of giving," Joe said. "In fact, this may be my last year here at this school. If I'm going to be a lawyer I need to move up into higher education."

Mandie stopped and looked up at him. "Oh, Joe, come to Mr. Chadwick's school in Asheville," she said excitedly. "The boys come over to visit our school for socials and things, and I'd get to see you now and then."

Joe stopped, looked down at her, and smiled. "That's a good idea, only Mr. Chadwick doesn't teach what I need to learn. You see, my parents want me to enroll in the university."

"University?" Mandie said with a loud gasp. "Why, the nearest one of those is a long way off."

"I know, but I have to go," Joe replied with a slight frown. "I won't like being so far away from home, but it won't be forever." He reached out and jerked the strings on her bonnet as he joked, "I have to get education so I can make lots of money in order to afford to marry and take care of you."

Mandie felt her face growing warm as she ducked away from him. "I suppose my mother will send me to one of those higher education schools somewhere soon because she wants me to learn to take care of the business when I come of age," she said. "It's too bad we can't just live in the country and farm."

"Farming is hard work," Joe said. "I'd rather do something else, like become a lawyer. But right now we'd better get moving if we're going to be back home by noon."

"You're right," Mandie agreed as they continued down the road toward the schoolhouse.

When the building finally came into view, Mandie stopped to stare at the one-room log cabin. She remembered there had been only sixteen pupils when she was attending school there. Mr. Tallant had divided the students into groups of four and kept them involved in four different subjects at the same time. Each group had children who were close in age and grade level. Mandie had been the youngest in Joe's group. She smiled when she remembered the notes passed between her and Joe right under Mr. Tallant's nose. She was certain the teacher had been aware of this but chose to ignore it.

"Coming?" Joe asked, bringing Mandie back to the present.

"Oh yes," Mandie said. She picked up Snowball and caught up with him. "I was just thinking about our classes here. It's so different at the Heathwoods' school in Asheville."

"That's what I'm talking about," Joe said as they walked toward the long front porch of the schoolhouse. "This is limited education here. Both of us need to go on to higher schools."

Mandie stepped onto the porch and tried to look through a window, but the shutters were closed. Snowball squirmed in her arms.

"I know the school is on harvest break, but when do you have to go back to class, Joe?" she asked.

"Next week," Joe said as he came up behind her. "Do you like going to a school where classes continue on through the school year without breaks, except for a few holidays?"

"Well, I suppose it's all right," Mandie said thoughtfully. "At least it's not broken up into pieces like the country schools where you have such long breaks you almost forget what you're learning."

"All the city schools go straight through, so once I leave here I'll be on the same schedule you're on," Joe said as he reached over and tried the door. "I suppose Mr. Tallant locked up the building because someone went inside one weekend not long ago and wrote all over the blackboard."

Mandie looked up at him and asked, "What did they write?"

Joe shrugged his thin shoulders and replied, "I don't know. He said it was lucky he found it and not one of the pupils."

"Does he know who did it?" Mandie asked.

"No, but he said he has a good idea," Joe said as he walked down the front steps. "Come on. We'd better get a move on."

Mandie followed, with Snowball still squirming in her arms. "Who do you think it was, Joe?" she asked as she looked back at the schoolhouse.

"I have no idea," Joe said, leading the way down the path to the road.

"Oh, Joe, you must have some idea," Mandie said as she came alongside him when they reached the main road.

Joe stopped, and Mandie paused by his side. He looked down at her and said, "Mandie, I don't know who it was."

"It must have been somebody who goes to school there," she said.

"Now, Mandie, I shouldn't have ever told you

anything about it," Joe said. "This is not a mystery you can solve, so let's forget about it."

Mandie frowned, but then gave him a big grin and said, "Well, you never know."

"I do know I'm not getting involved in it," Joe said.

"Why not?" Mandie asked.

"Because Mr. Tallant would have told us who he thought it was if he'd wanted us to know," Joe replied. "Do you want to go on to your father's house or not?"

"Oh yes, of course." Mandie began walking, and Joe caught up with her.

Mandie was silent as they continued down the road. *Who could have written on the blackboard?* she was wondering. *And what was it they wrote that caused Mr. Tallant to say he was glad he found it first?* She decided it must have been something terrible if he didn't want to tell his pupils what it said. All this was definitely a mystery, but she wasn't sure how she could solve it. She was only going to be here a few days, she thought. Besides, the school was closed and would not reopen until she had gone back to her school in Asheville.

"Where is your mind, Mandie?" Joe broke into her thoughts as he tweaked the long plait of blond hair hanging down her back.

Mandie whirled and darted away as she laughed and said, "In the future."

"Well then, bring it back to the present, because we are almost at your father's house," Joe told her.

"How are we going to get inside the house? You didn't bring any tools to open the door or windows," Mandie said.

"Tools?" Joe questioned her. "We can't just

break into a house like a burglar with tools and all."

"You said we'd find a way to get inside," Mandie reminded him.

"You'll have to help think up something," Joe said. "We didn't examine everything when we were there yesterday. Maybe there's a shutter with a missing hook or something, and we could use that to pry open a window."

"Or you could slide down the chimney like Snowball did in that house when those people kidnapped us, remember?" Mandie said with a big grin.

"Now *that* is one thing I'd never do for you," Joe said, frowning. "If you want someone to go down the chimney, then you do it."

"Oh, Joe, I was joking, but I do know the chimney is large enough for a person to get through," Mandie said. Snowball meowed, squirming to get down. She let him walk at the end of his leash, but she kept a tight hold on it.

When they walked around the bend, Mandie could see the house and barn in the distance. They both quickened their pace to get to the house. Her heartbeat quickened as she hurried through the open gate and stopped at the corner of the barn, hiding there so that anyone in the house could not see her. Joe came to stand beside her.

"I don't see anyone anywhere," Mandie whispered to him.

"I don't either, but someone could be in the house," Joe told her.

She turned to look up at Joe, and Snowball suddenly jerked the leash free. The cat rushed forward into the yard and began smelling around the house.

"Oh, Snowball!" Mandie said with a sigh. She

looked back at Joe and told him, "I'm going to have to get him."

"You'd better make it quick, because if anyone is in the house they might see you," Joe whispered back.

Mandie started to move forward and then paused. "I smell smoke. Is something on fire?" she asked as she sniffed the air and looked around.

"I smell it too," Joe agreed as he, also, took deep breaths.

Mandie looked around the corner to watch Snowball, who was now playing with a rotten apple in the yard near the house. When she looked up, she stopped and whispered quickly to Joe, "There's smoke coming out of the chimney!"

Joe came to her side. "Someone must be in the house, Mandie."

Mandie stomped her foot and said, "But I wanted to get inside the house!"

"You could always go up and knock on the door," Joe suggested.

"But how can we tell who is in there?" Mandie asked, still staring at the smoke.

"Well, we could creep up and look in the windows," Joe suggested as he looked at her.

"All right. Which way should we approach the house?" Mandie asked.

"From whichever way we won't be in full view of whoever is inside," Joe replied.

"There are windows on every side, so we'll just have to walk toward a corner," Mandie said. "Come on."

She led the way around to the front of the barn. She paused to look through the open door—there was no one inside. Continuing on, she darted from tree to tree as she watched the house. Joe followed. Snowball continued playing in the yard.

Mandie finally reached a corner of the house and began creeping toward the window on one side. Joe was right behind her. Just as she straightened up to look through the window she heard a sudden barking and screeching noise in the front yard.

Mandie and Joe both dropped to the ground.

"Snowball!" Mandie said in a loud whisper.

"And Samantha!" Joe added.

Mandie stayed where she was, expecting whoever was inside to open the door upon hearing the dog and the cat. She silently looked at Joe close behind her. She didn't hear a sound from the house.

Mandie could see the dog and cat had reached a standoff with each other, but the noise continued. Samantha continued barking and Snowball didn't give an inch of ground. He kept up his hissing and growling as he boxed the air with his front paw.

Finally Mandie whispered to Joe, "I don't believe anyone is inside."

"Someone had to build that fire to make smoke come out of the chimney," Joe reminded her.

"But maybe they've left," Mandie suggested.

"I have an idea," Joe said softly as he picked up a small pebble nearby. He threw it at the two animals, aiming it so it didn't hit either one.

Mandie watched as Samantha stopped and looked toward them. She immediately came running to her master. Snowball sat down and began washing his face.

"Snowball!" Mandie called softly to her white cat, but he ignored her.

"Samantha, go home. Home," Joe told his dog as he pointed to the road.

Samantha hesitated, looking back at Snowball and then at her master.

"Home, Samantha," Joe repeated.

Samantha wagged her tail as Joe patted her head. Then she raced off toward the road.

"Snowball," Mandie called softly again.

Snowball quit washing, looked at her, and then ran off in the direction Samantha had gone.

Mandie and Joe looked at each other and smiled.

"He is pursuing Samantha," Mandie said with a soft laugh.

"You know who would win if the two really got in a fight," Joe reminded her. "But maybe Samantha will ignore him if he stays away from her puppies."

"I hope so," Mandie whispered as the two crouched by the house.

"Shall we go home and see what happens?" Joe asked.

"After we look in the window," Mandie whispered. She slowly straightened up till her eyes were even with the bottom of the window. She squinted hard, but the curtain covering the window was too thick to see through.

Joe did the same thing, then he looked at her and shook his head.

Mandie stooped back down and whispered, "Let's try another window."

She led the way around to the window at the back of the house. Joe followed. That window was also covered on the inside. Mandie went to the other side, with Joe behind her. But there was also a curtain over the window there.

"That leaves the front," Mandie whispered as the two stooped below the window.

"Well, what are we waiting for?" Joe said in a soft voice.

Mandie began creeping around the house, then looked back at him and said, "Come on."

"Watch that bucket up there," Joe warned her. He pointed ahead.

Mandie saw it just in time to keep from banging into it. She knew it would have made a loud noise if she'd hit it. When she reached the front corner of the house, she paused to glance at the window on the porch.

"We'll have to step up onto the porch to look in that one," she warned Joe in a soft whisper.

"Right," Joe whispered back.

Mandie stood up just long enough to reach the porch and then crouched beneath the window. Joe followed. Glancing back at Joe, she slowly raised herself up enough to see through the window, and Joe did the same. But they discovered that this window was also heavily curtained.

"Oh shucks!" Mandie whispered as she dropped down to the floor and slid off into the yard. Joe came behind her.

"Give up?" Joe asked as they sat on the ground.

Mandie shook her head quickly and whispered, "No! I'll think of something."

"You could knock on the door," Joe suggested.

Mandie's face brightened as he said that. "I'll do just that," she said, determinedly rising and walking toward the steps of the porch.

Joe remained by the corner of the porch and watched.

If this was the only way to find out who was inside, she thought, then she would knock on the door. She was hoping no one would answer her knock, because she had no idea who it could be. *On the other hand,* she concluded, *someone has to be in the house, because smoke is coming out of the chimney.*

Mandie stepped up to the door and knocked loudly. She couldn't hear a sound inside the house. She knocked again and again without any results. She frowned and began beating on the door with her fists, but still no one answered.

Joe stood up and told her, "Let's go, Mandie. There's just not anybody in there."

Mandie looked at him with a frown and said, "I believe there is, and they just don't want to come to the door." She stepped down to join him in the yard. "But I'll come back."

"Yes, we can come back," Joe agreed, and the two slowly began walking toward the barn on their way to the road.

When they reached the corner of the barn, Mandie turned to look back. She gasped and grabbed Joe's arm. "Look! There's someone looking out the window!" she cried.

"Where?" Joe asked. "Oh, I see." The face at the window disappeared.

"But they didn't pull the curtain back enough for us to see who it is," Mandie said. "Maybe we should go back."

"If they didn't come to the door before, they're not going to come to the door if we go back, Mandie," Joe said. "We'll just have to figure out some way to see who it is."

"We can always watch the house. Whoever is in there has got to come outside now and then for different things," Mandie said.

"That's right," Joe agreed.

"I just don't understand why they wouldn't come

to the door," Mandie said as she continued staring at the window in the distance.

"I guess they just don't want to," Joe said. "Now do you want to go by the graveyard before we go back to my house?"

Mandie quickly looked at him. "Yes, I'd like to," she said.

"Then let's go. We still have to find that cat of yours, remember?" Joe said.

"Oh goodness, you're right," Mandie replied. "I had forgotten all about Snowball, and I don't see him anywhere around here."

"We can look for him after we walk up the mountain," Joe said.

The two climbed the narrow winding road to the top of the mountain. Mandie relived in her mind that day when her father's funeral procession had gone up this road. When she reached the cemetery at the end of the trail, she ran to her father's grave and dropped to her knees beside it. Her bonnet fell back on its strings.

"Oh, Daddy, I loved you so much!" she whispered as the tears streamed down her face. "I wish God could give you back to me! I miss you!" Her voice cracked, and Joe knelt beside her and put his arm around her shoulders.

"I love you, Mandie," Joe said softly, burying his cheek in her blond hair. He tightened his embrace.

Mandie suddenly realized what Joe had said, and she looked up at him through her tears. "I love you too, Joe," she replied in a shaky voice.

"I love everybody, but not like I love you, Mandie. It's a special kind of love," Joe tried to explain in a whisper as he continued holding her tight.

Mandie thought for a moment and then replied,

"I have a special kind of love for you too, Joe."

He handed her a handkerchief and she wiped her face. He helped her to her feet.

"I've always loved you, Mandie, and I'm serious when I say I won't outgrow it," Joe said, looking down into her reddened eyes. "I'm going on sixteen years old, not far from the marrying age, and when we reach that age I will tell you again that I love you and will ask you to become my wife."

Mandie could feel the love Joe radiated, and she answered seriously, "When we reach that age, I'll let you know my answer, Joe."

Joe smiled down at her and said, "That's good enough for me."

Mandie looked back at her father's grave and said, "I appreciate your putting flowers here all the time, Joe." There were wild flowers in a vase at the headstone.

"I think we'd better replace those. They've been here since before I went to Asheville, and they're kinda wilted, don't you think?" Joe said, stooping to pick up the vase. He carried it to the edge of the woods and threw the dead flowers away.

"I see something blooming down that way," Mandie said, pointing toward a pathway to their left.

"We'll get some water from the creek and fill this up with fresh flowers, and then we'd better look for Snowball," Joe told her.

"Oh, I wonder where he went," Mandie said with a big sigh. "You know, he still has his leash on and he could get tangled up on something. Let's hurry."

Mandie remembered her cat had run off in the same direction as Samantha, and she wondered if he might have followed the dog home.

Chapter 3 / Danger on the Mountain

Mandie and Joe searched the woods surrounding the cemetery for Snowball.

"Better to look for him up here first so we don't have to walk all the way back up the mountain to do it later," Mandie remarked as they shook every bush they came to, calling her cat's name.

They slowly made their way around the edge of the clearing. Now and then a squirrel ran across their path or birds put up a squabble overhead because their domain was being invaded. Mandie continued to call, "Snowball! Where are you?"

"I don't believe he is up here," Joe said with a loud sigh. They circled back to where they had begun.

"He probably followed Samantha home, but I guess we'd better look real good for him on our way down," Mandie said as she glanced around the clearing.

The two searched the pathway as they slowly

made their way back down the mountain. Mandie called Snowball's name now and then, but he was nowhere to be found. Once on the main road, Mandie and Joe hurried toward Joe's house.

"I sure hope Snowball is at your house," Mandie said, watching for the cat along the way.

"And I hope Samantha went home, too. More than likely she did," Joe replied as he slowed his long legs to keep pace with Mandie.

But when the two reached Joe's house, Mrs. Woodard informed them that neither animal had returned. "No, I haven't seen Samantha or Snowball since they followed y'all off," she said when Mandie and Joe found her at the back door.

"I suppose we'd better keep looking then," Joe said, glancing around the wide yard.

"No, first of all you two get into the kitchen and wash up. Dinner is on the table," the woman told them, then she looked at Joe and added, "Your father had to go on a call to the other side of the mountain, to the Mortons. Seems one of the young ones fell out of a tree and might have broken an arm or leg or something, so he ate in a hurry and left." She led the way through the door into the large kitchen.

"Those Mortons are always having accidents," Joe muttered as he waited for Mandie to wash at the sink.

"Hurry up now," Mrs. Woodard told them as she went on into the dining room.

"I sure hope we find Snowball and Samantha," Mandie said, drying her hands on a clean towel while Joe took his turn at the sink.

"Samantha never has gone far off before, so maybe she'll be back by the time we eat," Joe said.

"And I would imagine Snowball won't be far behind her," he added with a smile.

They joined Mrs. Woodard at the dining room table, where Mandie found corn on the cob, green beans, boiled potatoes, ham, tomatoes, and corn-bread.

"This sure is a lot of food," she remarked as they passed the food around.

"Well, you know how it is here in the country," Mrs. Woodard said, smiling at Mandie. "We just cook up everything for dinner in the middle of the day and eat leftovers at night."

"That's right," Mandie agreed as she placed a big slice of cornbread on her plate. "I've lived at that fancy school in the city so long, I'm glad to get back out to the country where things are normal."

"But you need that education, dear," Mrs. Woodard said, helping herself to the green beans. "And I know your mother will want you to go on from there to the university."

Mandie put down her fork as she heard this. Joe was going to the university next year, but no one had ever mentioned that she should go. "To the university?" she asked as she leaned forward.

"Yes, dear," Mrs. Woodard replied. "Someday you will have a lot of responsibility on your shoulders. With all that you will eventually inherit, you'll certainly need some business education."

"My mother has said I need education to handle business, but she has never mentioned the university," Mandie said, a slight frown on her face.

"I believe that's the only place you can learn about business, so she *must* be thinking about it," Mrs. Woodard said.

Mandie glanced at Joe and found him grinning at her.

"Maybe we'll catch up with each other there," Joe said as he put a forkful of potatoes in his mouth.

"We probably will, only you're two years older than I am and, therefore, you're two years ahead of me in school. I'll have to do some extra hard work to catch up with you before you leave the university," Mandie said, taking a sip of her coffee.

"Don't worry," Joe teased with a know-it-all attitude. "University education is four years long, so you'll *most likely* get there before I leave."

"Joe!" Mandie exclaimed. "I may be two years younger than you are, but I'm not four years dumber." She pursed her lips and straightened up in her chair.

Mrs. Woodard looked at the two and said, "If y'all will hurry up, you'll have time for a piece of chocolate cake before you look for the animals again."

"Chocolate cake!" the two exclaimed together.

"I know how much you like chocolate cake, Amanda," Mrs. Woodard said. She stood up and turned toward the kitchen. "I'll get it from the pie safe."

After Mrs. Woodard had left the room, Mandie and Joe looked at each other and began laughing.

"Your mother thought we were starting an argument, didn't she?" Mandie said.

"You're right," Joe replied. "She doesn't like arguments."

Mandie looked across the table at Joe with a serious expression on her face. "Oh, Joe, I could never argue with you," she said.

"And I couldn't argue with you, Mandie," Joe replied with a smile.

Then the two burst into laughter again just as Mrs. Woodard returned with the chocolate cake. She looked from one face to the other as she placed the plate on the table and removed the cover.

"M-m-m-m!" Mandie said, licking her lips. "Would it be all right, Mrs. Woodard, if I had a large slice? It looks so good!"

Mrs. Woodard looked at her as she began slicing the cake. "You may have half of it if you like, and I believe Joe would want the other half." She laughed.

"That's right. Half of it is mine," Joe declared. "However, I won't eat the whole half right now, because we've got to look for Samantha and Snowball, remember?"

"Oh yes, we'd better hurry," Mandie said as she accepted a plate with a large slice of the cake on it.

When they had finished, Mrs. Woodard insisted she didn't need help in clearing the table and that Mandie and Joe should start searching for the animals again immediately.

As soon as the two young people were outside, Mandie looked at Joe and said, "To the university, huh?"

Joe smiled down at her and said, "To the university."

The two searched the entire yard, the barn, the stable, and they even walked all the way to Mrs. Miller's house. No one was home there, and they found no sign of Samantha or Snowball.

"I just don't know where else to look unless we go back up the road toward your father's house,"

Joe said as they turned and started back toward the Woodards' house.

"I hate to waste all this time looking for Snowball. When I do find him, I'll make sure he doesn't get away from me again," Mandie said.

"It's not like Samantha to disappear for so long and not answer my call," Joe said as they approached the barn. "Let me look and be sure her puppies are all right."

Mandie followed him into the barn to see the puppies. They were in a pen in a corner of the barn, and a dog door nearby allowed Samantha to go in and out.

"Three brown ones and one white," Mandie remarked, bending to look at the little squealing animals. "They're so cute!"

"Cute, but a lot of trouble if Samantha doesn't show up soon," Joe replied as he stooped to rub their tiny heads. "I'm not sure they'd be able to eat yet, so I'd have to feed them milk." He stood up with a worried look on his face.

"Let's walk on back toward my father's house. Maybe we'll find one or both of them on the way," Mandie said.

"I sure hope so," Joe agreed as they walked from the barn toward the road.

They called their animals as they walked down the road and searched the bushes off to the side without getting any response. When they reached the fence around Mandie's father's land, Mandie quickly put out her hand to stop Joe.

"Listen, I hear something!" she said, looking about.

"What?" Joe asked.

"Snowball, where are you?" Mandie called

loudly. A faint noise came from the field of dried cornstalks nearby, and she rushed in that direction.

Joe followed as he called, "Samantha! Samantha!"

Mandie spotted a bunch of cornstalks moving, and she pushed her way through the rows of corn in that direction. There was Snowball! His red leash was wrapped around and around a cornstalk. "Snowball! How did you get into this mess?" she asked as she stooped to untangle the leash. Snowball meowed violently as he tried to pull free.

Joe bent to help her and broke away the dead stalks. "Pick him up," he told her. "Quick, Mandie, before he gets free and takes off again."

Mandie picked up her white cat just as Joe pulled his leash free.

"You've been a bad cat, Snowball," Mandie scolded him as she held him tight. "Maybe this will teach you a lesson."

"Now if I could only find Samantha," Joe said as he looked around.

Mandie and Joe searched the fields as they made their way toward her father's house, but there was no sign of Samantha.

Mandie and Joe paused by the barn to spy on the house. Smoke was still coming out of the chimney, but there was no sign of anyone in the yard or inside the barn.

"What do we do now?" Joe whispered to her.

"Let's go look through the windows and try to see inside again," Mandie suggested as she looked up at Joe standing close to her at the corner of the barn.

"All right, but we have to hurry. I've got to find Samantha," Joe told her.

Mandie quickly darted from tree to tree as she made her way toward the house. Joe followed. Just as they reached the side of the cabin they heard something hard ricochet off the tin roof of the house, and then they heard the sound of a loud gunshot.

"Down!" Joe ordered Mandie as he fell to the ground and pulled her with him. "That sounded like a bullet hitting the roof! But the person with the gun must be up on the mountain, because I didn't hear the shot until after the bullet hit the roof."

Mandie raised her head slightly to look around, but Joe immediately pushed it down.

"This way," Joe whispered as he held her by one hand while she grasped her cat with the other. Joe wriggled his way across the yard, pulling her with him. When they reached a large chestnut tree, Joe eased up to a stooping position to look around. Mandie, still holding his hand, did likewise. Snowball tried his best to get free from her arms, but she squeezed him close to her.

"I don't see anyone," Mandie whispered.

"The bullet came from the direction of the woods on the other side of the house," Joe told her as he squinted to see through the forest.

"Do you think they were shooting at *us*?" Mandie asked in a shaky voice, now that she realized the danger they were in.

"I don't know, but I am not staying around to find out," Joe whispered. "Let's lie down and crawl over to the next tree, then on to the barn. Then we'll be able to get to the other side of it and on into the cornfield. From there we can get out onto the road."

Mandie did as he told her. It was hard to follow him and hold on to her cat at the same time, but she was determined Snowball would not get away again. She tried to push her full skirts beneath her legs to keep them from getting torn on the rough ground. She knew her clothes would be ruined.

The two managed to reach the barn. They stopped long enough to look back while they were shielded by the building. There was no one in sight, and they had not heard another shot.

"Let's get out to the road," Joe told her as he continued quickly through the cornfield. Mandie stayed close behind him.

Once on the road they paused for breath.

"Whew! That was breathtaking!" Mandie said with a gasp.

"It could have been life-taking," Joe reminded her. "I can't figure out what was going on, whether someone was shooting at us or at the house, or maybe at whoever could be inside the house."

"I didn't hear anything but the bullet hitting the roof then the shot. They must have been a good ways off," Mandie said, holding Snowball close. "Do you want to go looking for them?"

"I've got to find Samantha," Joe reminded her.

"She could be over that way," Mandie suggested, pointing toward where the shot had come from.

Joe thought about that for a moment and then replied, "I know, but the only way we can go in that direction is to go up to the cemetery and come down the other side of the mountain. Whoever is over there would be sure to see us."

"Let's go back to your house and get your rifle. Then if they shoot at us again you can shoot back," Mandie said.

"I suppose it would be a good idea to get my rifle. If someone saw us with a gun they might not be so quick to shoot. Come on. Let's go," Joe said as he hurried off down the road.

Mandie's short legs worked hard to keep up with Joe's long stride, and when they reached his house she plopped down on the porch steps. Joe looked at her and smiled. "Sorry. I went too fast," he said. "Stay right here and rest. I'll get my rifle and ask my mother if Samantha has come back." He started around the corner of the house.

"Wait," Mandie said, quickly getting to her feet to follow him. "I need to do something with Snowball. I don't want to have to carry him back with me."

"Take him up to your room and shut him in. I'll meet you back down here," Joe told her.

"Don't be too long. Whoever it was who shot at us will be gone, and we won't know which direction he went," Mandie called to him as she turned back to go inside the house.

"I won't," Joe promised, continuing toward the backyard.

Mandie wondered where Mrs. Woodard was as she entered the front hallway and went on up the stairs. She didn't hear anyone in the house.

She pushed open the door to her room and went inside. After she had closed it, she set Snowball down. As she took off his leash she told him, "You are going to stay right here this time. I'll be back soon."

Snowball looked up at her, jumped up on the bed, and began washing his face. Mandie glanced back at him and then closed the door. She knew he would be taking a nap.

As Mandie came downstairs, she could hear

Mrs. Woodard and Joe talking clear back in the kitchen, so she went to join them.

"I gave the puppies some milk in a pan and they managed to lap it up, so I suppose they will be all right for the time being—but we must find Samantha," Mrs. Woodard was saying from where she sat by the cookstove.

Joe was standing by the table, holding his rifle. "I know," he said. "We're going to keep looking for her."

"What do you need with that gun?" Mrs. Woodard asked.

Mandie stepped forward and replied, "Someone shot at us, Mrs. Woodard."

"Shot at y'all?" Mrs. Woodard quickly questioned.

"Well, we're not sure they were shooting at *us* exactly, but someone fired a gun while we were down at Mandie's old house looking for Samantha," Joe explained.

"Oh, dear, maybe y'all had better not go down that way for a while," Mrs. Woodard said as she stood up.

"Oh, Mama, we'll be careful," Joe promised, and holding up his rifle he added, "You know that I do know how to use this rifle."

"Yes, but you would need to use it first, remember," his mother warned him. "And I don't think you ought to go around shooting at people first."

"But we won't even go near the house down there this time," Joe said. "We'll just go looking everywhere else for Samantha."

"We'll be careful," Mandie told her.

"Maybe you ought to wait until your father gets

home, then he could go with you," Mrs. Woodard suggested.

"What time is he coming home?" Joe asked.

"I just don't know. When he goes off doctoring people there always seems to be another he needs to see, and he never worries about getting back home," she said. "One of these days I'm going to make him take some time off for himself and for his family."

Joe stepped forward to put an arm around his mother's shoulders. "Mama, you've been around him longer than I have and you know you can't make him do anything. Anyway, don't worry about us. We won't be gone long. I promise." Joe turned toward the door.

"Yes, please be careful, son," Mrs. Woodard said, and then looking at Mandie added, "And, Amanda, be sure you don't take any chances with danger, or your grandmother will skin me alive." She smiled.

Mandie smiled back as she followed Joe to the door and said, "Don't worry, Mrs. Woodard. I don't think you'd look pretty skinned alive."

Mrs. Woodard laughed as the two left the room.

Once outside Mandie and Joe stopped to plan their route.

"We promised we wouldn't go near your father's house, so we have to go up the mountain by the cemetery," Joe told her.

"All right. That's what we had planned anyway," Mandie agreed.

"And we'll have to hurry," Joe reminded her as he looked down at her dirty dress, then at his own soiled clothes.

"You know, your mother didn't even notice that

we were all messed up, did she?" Mandie asked as they stood there in the yard.

"It's good she didn't, because she would have been upset sure enough then," Joe said. "Now let's get going."

As they hurried along the road, Joe explained to Mandie that he would have to at least whistle for Samantha now and then in order to try to find her.

"But since I have this rifle, I think we're safe," Joe said. "I'll just whistle real fast, and we'll keep moving. If she's around she'll hear us and come to me."

"I sure hope so," Mandie said. She wouldn't admit it to Joe, but she was a little afraid. Whoever had fired that other shot could very well shoot at them without being seen. Her eyes carefully searched the road as they walked on.

Chapter 4 / Miss Abigail

Mandie and Joe walked slowly enough to search the bushes, and Joe whistled now and then, but there was still no sign of Samantha.

When they reached the road that turned off toward the schoolhouse, Mandie quickly put her hand on Joe's arm to stop him. "Maybe we should look around the schoolhouse for Samantha," she suggested. "She could have gone down that way."

"You're right," Joe agreed as he turned down the road. "Come on," he called, and Mandie followed.

They stopped a couple of times for Joe to whistle. When the schoolhouse came into sight, they paused once more. Joe puckered his lips to whistle but suddenly stopped without making a sound. Mandie quickly looked in the direction he was facing. She saw a woman carrying a small picnic basket as she left the school building.

"Is that—?" Mandie paused as she squinted in the sunshine.

"Miss Abigail Durham," Joe finished for her. "Yes, that's Miss Abigail Durham, and I don't believe she saw us."

"Well, how did she get inside the schoolhouse when it is supposed to be locked?" Mandie asked.

"Let's just go see," Joe replied.

They watched until Miss Abigail Durham had disappeared down the pathway behind the building, and then they walked slowly forward.

"The door is open," Mandie said as they stepped up onto the porch.

"Yes," Joe agreed.

Mandie peered in through the doorway, and Joe came right behind her. They were both surprised to see Mr. Tallant sitting at his desk doing some kind of paperwork. Mandie and Joe looked at each other, both surprised.

Mandie walked on inside. "Hello, Mr. Tallant," she said loudly as she walked forward. "Remember me? I'm Mandie Shaw."

Joe set his rifle down on the porch and followed. Mr. Tallant looked up in surprise and got to his feet. A big smile spread across his handsome, middle-aged face. "Amanda Shaw!" he exclaimed as he came to take her hand. "My, my, I do believe you've grown a little bit since you left here."

"Oh yes, Mr. Tallant, I'm going on fourteen years old now," she said with a big smile as she stretched to her full height.

"And, Joe, how are you?" the schoolmaster greeted Joe.

"Fine, Mr. Tallant," Joe replied. "We're looking

for my dog, Samantha. You haven't seen her, have you?"

Mr. Tallant thought for a moment and then said, "Don't believe I have since school let out."

Mandie glanced past Mr. Tallant to his desk. She saw a plate with a slice of coconut cake on it and a pot of coffee on the stove nearby. *So*, she thought, *Miss Abigail Durham has brought Mr. Tallant some food. Hm-m-m!*

"Mandie got out of school for a few days to visit with us," Joe explained.

"Because I wanted to find out if those people have moved out of my father's house. Do you know, Mr. Tallant?" Mandie asked quickly.

"No, I'm sorry, Amanda, but I haven't seen any of those people in a long time. Irene quit school quite a while back," he explained. "You know I live in the other direction, so I don't ever go by your father's house. Did someone say the house was empty?"

Joe spoke up. "It looks deserted. The weeds and the grass have all grown up, and there's no sign of any livestock," he explained.

Mandie looked at him and added, "But not exactly deserted, because we saw smoke coming out of the chimney."

"That's strange," Mr. Tallant said.

"We thought we saw someone peeking out the window at us from behind the curtain, but when we knocked on the door there was no sound at all. No one answered. We tried to open the door, but it was locked," Mandie explained.

"I'd say if there was smoke coming out of the chimney, someone had to be inside and they had a fire going in the fireplace," Mr. Tallant said.

"And someone shot off a gun while we were down there a little while ago," Mandie added.

Mr. Tallant quickly looked at her and said, "Oh, my goodness! I'd advise you two to stay away from there." He turned to Joe and asked, "You're not planning on going back to that house, are you?"

"No, sir, we're going up the road to the cemetery so we can come down the other side in order to search for Samantha," Joe explained.

Mandie walked across the room and paused at the old, scarred wooden desk where she had sat while attending school here. Those had been happy days. Her father had still been alive then, and she had lived with him. She felt tears beginning to fill her eyes. Quickly walking across the room, she went to stand at a window and looked outside. She breathed deeply to calm her emotions.

"Ready to go on?" Joe called across the room to her.

Mandie turned and, not looking directly at him, she replied, "Right."

"I'm glad you stopped by, Amanda," Mr. Tallant said. "Do come back again."

"I will, Mr. Tallant," Mandie managed to say as she smiled and looked up at him.

She followed Joe out the door. As she caught up with him in the school yard, he gave her a big grin and said, "Hm-m-m!"

"What?" Mandie asked.

"So Miss Abigail brought Mr. Tallant a piece of cake to go with his coffee," Joe said mischievously. "Interesting!"

"It sure is interesting," Mandie agreed. "She must like him, but does he like her? I always had the idea Mr. Tallant would stay an old bachelor because he was too shy to talk to women."

Joe laughed and said, "Now that's the truth. He is always nice and perfectly polite around women, but I don't remember him ever being interested in a single one."

"So you think Miss Abigail is the pursuer in this case?" Mandie asked.

"I just don't know," Joe said. "I've always heard she had a sad love story in her past, and that she would never look at another man, but who knows now?"

"Yes, it sure looks like she's interested in Mr. Tallant, or she wouldn't be bringing him cake," Mandie said. "And somehow she had to know he was here even though the school was on break and he wasn't supposed to be here."

"Well, most people around here know that when the school is on break Mr. Tallant never stops work. He's always doing something—paperwork, painting, cleaning, or something—all the time," Joe said. He quickly changed the subject and said, "And I think we'd better get busy doing something, like looking for Samantha."

He started toward the road, and Mandie caught up with him when he paused long enough to whistle for his dog. There was no response, so they walked on.

"Will you let me know what develops between Miss Abigail and Mr. Tallant?" Mandie asked as they continued down the road.

Joe looked down at her with a big grin and said, "Mandie Shaw, you are a *busybody*, did you know that?"

Mandie pursed her lips and returned the look.

"Well, aren't you interested in such an unusual situation?" she asked.

Joe shrugged and replied, "I'm more interested in finding my dog right now."

"Yes, for right now we need to find Samantha, but I'd like to know what goes on later between the two," Mandie said.

"But nothing may go on between them later. How do we know whether they're even interested in each other? Maybe Miss Abigail brought the cake because she was just being a good neighbor," Joe replied as they walked on.

"Miss Abigail just being a good neighbor and going to the school to see Mr. Tallant alone, without anyone else being around? Impossible!" Mandie told him. "It took a lot of nerve on her part or a lot of encouragement from Mr. Tallant for her to do that."

Joe looked down at her as they went on down the road. "Well, whatever caused her to take him cake is none of our business, Mandie Shaw, and don't you go making a mystery out of it, because if you do, I refuse to become involved," he said.

"All right, Joe Woodard, if you are not interested, forget about it," Mandie said. "I'll find out for myself."

Joe only shrugged. As they came to the main road he stopped to whistle for Samantha, but without any results. They continued following the road up the mountain to the cemetery.

At the top of the mountain, Mandie glanced in the direction of her father's grave, but she bit her lip and continued on with Joe down the other side. This road was seldom used. The underbrush was thick, and in some places, it was hard to walk through without getting scratched by limbs and briars.

"I don't see how Samantha could have ever got through this place without getting tangled up on something," Mandie said as she pulled long, running vines with briars away from her full skirts. "We'll be lucky if we can make it to the bottom."

Joe smiled back at her as he said, "And just think. We have to come back this way." He used the butt of his rifle to push back bushes for her.

Mandie thought about that for a moment and then replied, "Unless we just walk by the house and go on down the main road."

"And be exposed in the open yard down there where someone could get a good aim at us?" Joe questioned as he continued on.

"I imagine whoever was shooting has gone on by now," Mandie said.

"We'll just find out," Joe said, stopping in front of her. "I need to whistle for Samantha in case she is anywhere near here."

Mandie looked up at him as he pursed his lips and gave a shrill whistle. The two stood there silently waiting to see if there was any reaction to the sound, either from whoever had been shooting before or from Samantha. The only noise after the echo died away was the twitter of birds in the trees.

They went on down the overgrown trail and stopped when they came within sight of the log cabin below. Staying hidden behind bushes, they looked down at the house, but they couldn't see or hear anything.

"There's still smoke coming out of the chimney," Mandie whispered, even though they were too far away to be heard by anyone near the house.

"Which means whoever is inside must have

wood to burn—but when do they come outside to get it?" Joe replied as he watched.

"Maybe they have a whole room full of wood and don't have to come outside," Mandie said, squinting to see the front door of the house.

"But we didn't see any sign of anyone having chopped wood," Joe replied. He looked around the area where they stood. "Anyhow, I've got to find Samantha." He suddenly startled Mandie with a loud whistle that echoed through the woods.

Suddenly a shot rang out on the mountain above them. Joe quickly put his arm around Mandie and held his rifle tightly in his other hand.

"Now we have to go on down this side, because whoever is shooting is behind us," Mandie said in a hoarse whisper as she leaned closer to Joe.

"Yes, and I think we'd better hurry," Joe said as he started forward, holding Mandie's hand while he beat back the bushes from the pathway.

Hurriedly pressing through the underbrush, Mandie didn't mind the bushes scratching because she had only one thought: to get to the bottom of the path and onto the main road before the person shooting could catch up with them.

The two reached the yard of the house and circled around the barn to go through the cornfields. Another shot sounded behind them, and they could see the bullet bounce off the tin roof of the house.

"I don't think they're shooting at us. They seem to be aiming at the house," Joe whispered as they stood behind the corner of the barn.

Even as he spoke, another bullet hit the tin roof of the house.

"I wonder who is inside the house and why they

are being shot at," Mandie said as they continued to watch.

"We must have passed whoever is up there," Joe remarked. "Therefore, if they had wanted to shoot at us, they would have done it when we were close to them."

The two waited for a while, but no more shots were fired. And nothing moved around the house. There was complete silence.

Finally unable to remain still any longer, Mandie whispered, "Maybe Samantha has gone home by now."

Joe looked at her as they stood there by the barn and replied, "I suppose we could go see if she has turned up at home."

As they edged their way toward the cornfield, Mandie whispered again, "I have an idea. Why don't we come back here after dark? Then we would be able to see inside the house if whoever is in there has a lamp lit."

"We could if they don't close the shutters for the night," Joe agreed. He pushed aside dried cornstalks to make a pathway through the field.

When they reached the main road they paused to listen once more, and Joe whistled again for Samantha.

Mandie squinted her blue eyes to look up and down the winding road. Nothing seemed to be moving anywhere.

"Joe, maybe Samantha went on past your house when she left us and has gone off down the road in the other direction," Mandie suggested as they stood there.

"I've never known her to wander off in that direction, but of course, she could have," Joe replied.

"You know, this is really frustrating. I know now how you feel when Snowball disappears." He looked down at her and grinned.

Mandie grinned mischievously back at him and said, "I'm glad you finally understand."

"But this is the first time Samantha has gone off like this, and your cat is always running away—and getting into trouble, too," Joe teased.

"Speaking of Snowball, I just thought of something," Mandie said with a gasp. "I didn't tell your mother that he was shut up in my room. She might go up there for something and let him out accidentally."

"We'd better hurry," Joe said. "We don't want to have to look for two animals."

"No, we don't," Mandie agreed.

When the two arrived back at Joe's house, they found Mrs. Woodard sitting in a swing under a tree in the backyard. She was embroidering a pillowcase.

"That is beautiful," Mandie said, looking down at the tiny rosebuds Mrs. Woodard was making on the white cloth. "Is that a special present for someone?"

"Thank you, Amanda," Mrs. Woodard said, looking up at her with a smile and then giving Joe a glance. "I hope one day it will be a special present for someone special, that is, if Joe ever gets done with all his education and finds time to get married."

Mandie looked at Joe and found him staring at her.

"Oh, I'll find time to get married a few years from now if the bride is named Mandie Shaw," he said teasingly.

Mandie couldn't think of an answer fast enough, so she changed the subject. "I forgot to tell you, Mrs. Woodard, that I left Snowball in my room while we were gone this time," she said, not looking directly at the woman.

"I know, Amanda," Mrs. Woodard said. "I let him down into the kitchen with me for a while, but when I came out here I thought I'd better put him back in your room so he couldn't run off somewhere." Turning to Joe, she said, "I see you haven't found Samantha."

"No, ma'am, and we only came by to see if she had come home. We're planning to go up the road in the other direction to look for her," Joe explained.

"I think you'd better hurry then, so you'll be back in time for supper," Mrs. Woodard said. "Your father should be back before then."

"We'll hurry," Joe promised as he and Mandie started to walk around the house. He stopped and called back, "Mother, if Samantha does come home while we're gone, would you please shut her up in the barn till we get back?"

"Of course, now y'all hurry," Mrs. Woodard replied as she began working on her embroidery again.

Mandie and Joe walked along the main road in the opposite direction from where they had been. They searched the fields and Joe called his dog, but there was no response. This area was more or less deserted. Most of the land was uncultivated, and there was only one small farmhouse within several miles of Joe's home.

"You see, there's not much on this stretch of the road, and Samantha wouldn't have any reason to wander off this way," Joe remarked as they walked on.

"Well, I can think of a good reason. Samantha could have chased a rabbit up this way. I've seen several in the fields since we left your house," Mandie told him.

"I suppose so, but we feed her good, and she has been staying close to home with the puppies now," Joe said. He stopped to whistle, and Mandie slowed down to glance around.

"Look! There's someone behind us coming this way," she told Joe.

He also looked back. "I believe that's Mr. Tallant's cart. He's probably going home."

"Looks like he has someone with him," Mandie said, her hand shading her eyes as she squinted in the bright sunshine.

"Yes, he does," Joe agreed.

"And I do believe it's Miss Abigail!" Mandie exclaimed as the cart came nearer.

The two waited until the cart caught up with them. Mandie was right, it was Miss Abigail Durham with the teacher. Mr. Tallant called as he drove on, "Still looking for your dog?"

Miss Abigail didn't speak. She tilted her head so the wide-brimmed hat she wore hid her face.

"If I see her I'll let you know," the schoolmaster replied as he passed on.

As soon as the cart and its occupants were out of sight around the bend in the dusty road, Mandie laughed and said, "That was very interesting!" She looked up at Joe, who was staring after the cart.

"I suppose you could call it that," Joe said as he shrugged his thin shoulders and began walking ahead.

Mandie caught up with him and said, "I wonder where they are going. Mr. Tallant lives down this road, doesn't he?"

"So?" Joe asked as he looked down at her.

"So do you suppose Mr. Tallant was taking Miss Abigail home with him?" Mandie asked.

Joe frowned as he replied, "I do declare, Mandie, you are a *busy* busybody."

Mandie paused to stomp her foot and asked, "Well, do you think he was taking her home with him or not?"

"Evidently, since she was in the cart with him. He is taking her somewhere," Joe replied, stopping to look down at her. He whirled around, whistled sharply, and moved on up the road.

Mandie was becoming irritated with Joe and she felt he was losing patience with her. The weather was hot for September, and she was tired. She slowly started to follow Joe.

"Joe, I don't think I can marry you when we grow up," she called to him.

Joe stopped instantly and looked back. "Why?" he asked as she caught up with him.

Mandie looked up at his serious face and explained, "I don't think you would put up with my curiosity about people and everything. My imagination runs wild sometimes."

Joe quickly reached for her hand and squeezed it tight as he looked down into her blue eyes. "Mandie, nobody is perfect," he said. "And I certainly wouldn't want you to be perfect. I love you just the way you are."

"But if you were around me all the time you might change your mind," Mandie said with a frown.

"You want your father's house back, don't you? I've always promised I'd get it back for you if you'd marry me, remember?" Joe said.

"But you don't even know for sure that you could get it back," Mandie reminded him.

"I'll find a way," Joe said emphatically. "I'm going to be a lawyer, and I'll learn all the legal angles. I'll get it back for you."

Mandie cleared her throat and asked, "Even if I don't marry you?"

"Oh, Mandie, let's stop this crazy talk right now," Joe said, squeezing her hand tighter. "We'll settle all this when we get old enough to marry."

"When that time comes, just remember I warned you about my imagination," Mandie said with a nervous laugh.

"I'll always remember every little thing about you, Mandie," Joe replied.

This time, Mandie was the one who said, "Let's find Samantha." They moved on.

Sometimes she felt as though Joe could read her thoughts. But she didn't want him to know her feelings right now, because she was thinking that marrying him would never work.

Chapter 5 / Another Mystery

After walking two miles up the road, Joe finally decided they should go home. Samantha was nowhere to be found. They had not seen anyone else after Mr. Tallant passed them on the deserted road and, therefore, could not inquire whether Samantha had been in the area.

"I give up," Joe said with a disappointed sigh after he had stopped to whistle for his dog.

Mandie looked up at him. She could feel his worry. Samantha was dear to Joe, just as Snowball was to her. She knew how it would be to lose an animal so dear to her heart. She remembered the time Snowball had been lost and come limping home, injured and half dead.

"I'm sorry, Joe," she said, reaching for his hand. "Don't give up. Samantha will come home, I'm sure, or we'll find her somewhere. After we eat supper and it gets dark, we are going back to my father's house, remember? Maybe we'll find her then."

"Thanks, Mandie," Joe said, smiling down at her. "You're right. I won't give up, but we'll have to go home now. It's getting late."

When they reached the back road to the school, Mandie suggested, "Let's go check around the schoolhouse one more time since we're almost at it."

"Well, I suppose we could," Joe agreed, so the two turned off, onto the road toward the schoolhouse.

As they passed a lane going off to their right, Mandie remarked, "Nimrod used to live down that trail—you know, the fellow who was sweet on Irene when I was living at home with my father."

"As far as I know he still lives there," Joe replied as they walked on.

"He was always hanging around our house," Mandie said. "He's a lot older than Irene, but she seemed to like him." She paused and then added, "What has happened to Irene and Etta and Zack Hughes? Are they living in my father's house anymore."

"Maybe Zack got a job some other place and they moved away," Joe suggested.

"But then who could be in my father's house?" Mandie said, puzzled.

"We'll find out," Joe assured her.

They walked past the pathway leading to Miss Abigail's house and then came out at the back of the school building. Joe stopped and whistled for Samantha several times without any response.

Mandie led the way to the front of the building as the two kept a constant watch for any sign of the dog. She glanced at the front door and was surprised to see it was partly open.

"Look," she said, hurrying up onto the front

porch. "The door is open again."

Joe looked toward her and said, "Mr. Tallant must have forgotten to lock it."

Mandie reached forward and pushed it all the way open, then stepped inside. Joe followed.

"There's nobody here," Joe said.

"No, but look at the blackboard!" Mandie exclaimed. She walked over and saw the crude handwriting across the board. "It says 'Miss Abigail' and the next word is smeared. I can't read it."

Joe stood behind her and gazed at the writing. "It says 'Miss Abigail' all right, but I have no idea what the messed-up word is," he said.

"Now I wonder who would write Miss Abigail's name up there," Mandie said, stepping forward to squint at the illegible word. "I wish I knew what the other word was meant to be."

"I'm sure that isn't Mr. Tallant's handwriting, so someone must have found the door unlocked and just come in," Joe said.

Mandie quickly looked at him and said, "You told me about someone writing on the blackboard before, that Mr. Tallant started locking the door after that. It must be the same person."

"Maybe," Joe said. "But I don't know why Mr. Tallant would leave the door unlocked."

"Maybe he forgot," Mandie said with a big smile. "Remember, we saw him riding down the road with Miss Abigail? She probably came back to the schoolhouse and left with him from here."

Joe picked up the eraser and quickly wiped the writing off the blackboard.

"Joe, why are you doing that?" Mandie demanded.

"You're making a mystery out of it, and I just

solved the mystery—it no longer exists," Joe said with a grin as he dusted the chalk from his hands.

"That doesn't just wipe out the fact that someone did write on the blackboard," Mandie argued.

"Well anyway, no one will know about it but us, so whoever wrote that on the blackboard won't get the satisfaction of having Mr. Tallant discover it," Joe explained. "I'm sure they did it out of meanness."

"But if we could find out who did it, we could tell Mr. Tallant, and they would be in trouble if they did it again," Mandie replied.

"Oh, come on, Mandie, let's go home," Joe said, turning to leave the room. "Whoever wrote that is probably long gone by now."

Mandie followed him out and waited while he pulled the door shut.

"I can't lock it because the key is not here," Joe said, examining the lock. "Anyway, Mr. Tallant wouldn't be able to get back inside if I locked it and took the key."

"Do you think Mr. Tallant has the key but just forgot to lock it?" Mandie asked. She glanced back at the closed door as they walked across the porch.

"He probably keeps the key in some safe place around here," Joe said.

He went down the steps and Mandie followed.

"If we could find it, then we could lock the door and put the key back in its hiding place," Mandie suggested.

"No, Mandie, we're going home right now," Joe said, determinedly walking on.

"All right, but we can come back by here when we go to my father's house tonight," Mandie said as she paused to look back.

"Mandie, come on," Joe said as he looked back

at her. "Or I'm going home and leaving you here."

"I'm coming." Mandie said, quickly catching up with him.

She was wondering if this incident could be connected to whatever was going on at her father's house, but since Joe was so stubborn about it, she wouldn't even mention it to him. She'd figure out a way to solve the mystery.

The two walked down the schoolhouse lane in front and reached the main road. Joe whistled now and then for his dog. Mandie watched the fields and bushes, hoping to see someone who might have been in the school building. They ended up at Joe's house without any results.

"Let's check on the puppies," Joe suggested as they came into the yard.

"Maybe Samantha is back," Mandie said.

They walked around the house to the barn, but when they looked in on the puppies, Samantha was not there. Joe hung his rifle on the gun rack nearby.

"No Samantha," Joe said with a big sigh.

Mandie glanced down through the long barn. Dr. Woodard's horse was in the last stall. "Your father is home," she said, motioning toward the animal.

"Yes, he is. Let's go inside the house," Joe said.

They found Dr. and Mrs. Woodard both in the kitchen. The doctor was leafing through a medical book as he sat by a window, and his wife was finishing up supper.

Joe just looked at his mother, and she immediately read his thoughts. "No sign of Samantha," she said.

Joe shook his head.

"But we'll look some more after supper," Mandie told her.

Dr. Woodard spoke from across the room, "Seems strange that Samantha would just run off like that."

"Yes, sir. She never has before," Joe replied.

"Well now, y'all get yourselves cleaned up. I'm putting the food on the table," Mrs. Woodard said, taking a pan of hot cornbread out of the oven.

"You first," Joe told Mandie.

"Thanks," Mandie said as she left the room and hurried down the back hallway to the bathroom. She removed her bonnet and washed her face and hands. Then she picked up a brush lying on the washstand and quickly brushed back the hair around her face. She was wearing it in one long plait, and it would take too long to unbraid it, brush it out, and then redo it.

Mandie quickly returned to the kitchen, and Joe left to clean up. "What can I do to help?" she asked Mrs. Woodard.

"If you would just slice up the cornbread, that would be a great help," Mrs. Woodard told her, pointing to the pan on the stove top as she ladled food out of the pots in front of her, Mandie began cutting the bread.

When Joe returned to the kitchen, they had everything ready and waiting on the dining room table. After they sat down, Mandie realized she was awfully hungry. She glanced at Joe across the table and noticed he was only nibbling on his food. She knew he was worried about his dog, but she couldn't think of anything to say that would help him.

Dr. Woodard broke the silence. "I told your mother," he said to Joe, "that I'll have to go across the other side of the mountain as soon as we finish eating. The Guytons sent word their daughter, Gretchen, may be coming down with the measles.

I believe she goes to your school."

"Yes, sir, she does," Joe replied. "I'm sorry she is sick. Aren't the measles contagious?"

"Indeed they are," his father replied as he sipped his coffee. "I just hope this is not the beginning of an outbreak. The stuff can be deadly."

"It sure can," Mrs. Woodard agreed as she passed the bowl of beans down the table to Mandie and told her, "Have some, dear."

"Thank you, Mrs. Woodard," Mandie replied and helped herself to the beans. "I don't believe I remember anyone named Gretchen Guyton when I was going to school here."

"The Guytons just moved here this spring," Dr. Woodard explained.

"She's a beautiful girl—dark, curly hair and hazel eyes," Mrs. Woodard remarked.

"Beautiful?" Mandie questioned, looking at Joe.

"I'd say pretty, but far, far behind in her education," Joe said, setting down his cup of coffee.

"Why?" Mandie asked in surprise.

"Her family has been living in the mountains of Tennessee where there was no school near enough for her to attend," Joe explained.

"That's why they moved here, so Gretchen could go to school," Mrs. Woodard added as she sliced her piece of bread open and inserted a lump of butter. She looked at Mandie and asked, "Now tell me, dear, did y'all find out what is going on at your father's house?"

Mandie laid down her fork and frowned as she replied, "No, ma'am, not really. Someone shot again, but they're shooting at the house."

"Shooting at the house?" Dr. Woodard asked, looking at Joe.

"I had my rifle," Joe told his father. "It seemed to me they were shooting at the roof of Mandie's father's house and not at us, so I didn't have to use it."

"Now why would someone shoot at the roof of a house?" Dr. Woodard asked as he sipped his coffee.

"That's part of the mystery, Dr. Woodard," Mandie told him. "We don't know whether it was someone shooting at the house because there is someone in the house or someone just trying to scare us."

"Maybe y'all shouldn't go back down there," Dr. Woodard said.

"Oh, please, Dr. Woodard, we'll be extra careful. That's the reason I came here, remember? To visit my father's house and find out whether anyone is living in it or not." Mandie looked at him, pleading.

"I don't think we were in danger, and we do have to find Samantha. The last we saw of her was down there," Joe explained.

"I don't like the idea of y'all going back alone, but I have to go to the Guytons," Dr. Woodard said. "Just promise me that you will be extra careful."

"Yes, sir, we will," Mandie promised.

"I'll take my rifle with me when I go back," Joe said. "That way anyone who sees us will know we have it, and that we can shoot back if they try shooting at us."

"Oh goodness, I'll be worried to death until y'all get back," Mrs. Woodard said.

"If we can find her, Samantha is a good watchdog, you know," Joe said, "and we just have to find her."

Dr. Woodard stood up and said, "I've got to hurry now. Just remember to be careful and don't stay gone too long or your mother will be worried." He reached to pat Joe's shoulder.

"Yes, sir," Joe said as he rose from the table.

Dr. Woodard gave his wife a quick kiss on the cheek, grabbed his medical bag from the sideboard, put on his hat, and went out the back door.

"I'll feed the puppies some more milk," Mrs. Woodard said as she and Mandie rose. "Y'all go ahead so you can get on back home."

"I need to give Snowball something to eat," Mandie told her.

"Don't worry about that. I'll feed him also. I'd rather y'all go on and get back early."

"Thank you," Mandie said. "I'll get my bonnet and be right back."

"And I'll get my rifle from the barn," Joe said, going out the back door.

Mandie hurried to the bathroom, where she had hung her bonnet. She quickly put it on and got back to the kitchen as Joe came in with his gun.

"I'm ready," Mandie told him.

Mrs. Woodard reached to embrace Mandie and said, "Please be careful," and then she looked up at Joe and repeated her warning, "Joe, take care of Amanda."

"Yes, ma'am," the two young people said at the same time as they went out the back door.

Supper had been late, and the sun disappeared early behind the huge North Carolina mountains. Dusk was already falling over the countryside. Joe called his dog's name now and then, and Mandie squinted to look into the bushes as they walked along the road.

"I sure will be glad when we find Samantha," Mandie said. "I'm worried about what could be happening to her."

Joe glanced down at Mandie and said, "So am I—I keep imagining all kinds of things. A wild animal could have injured her, or she could have been caught in an animal trap, or someone could have stolen her—but I doubt that could have happened. Samantha does not make friends with strangers, and it would have to be a stranger who would steal her. I don't think anyone I know would take her, because they would realize she belongs to me."

"I'm hoping she just chased a rabbit or something and is too far away to hear you calling her," Mandie said. "And I'm also hoping whoever is inside my father's house has a lamp lit so we can see inside."

"Maybe," Joe said.

As they approached the log cabin, the two stopped beside the barn to look across the yard.

"I don't see anyone outside," Mandie whispered. "But I don't see a light inside either."

"Let's just circle around and come up at the back door. Then we can try to see through the window there," Joe said.

He led the way and the two crept through the bushes, finally coming into the backyard. Slipping from tree to tree for cover, they managed to come up under the back window.

"I still don't see any light from the inside," Mandie said as they huddled beneath the window.

"Let's slowly get up and look in," Joe said.

The two straightened up. The curtain had been drawn aside and Mandie could see through the glass pane. There was no lamp lit inside, but there was light from the fire in the huge fireplace. Her eyes quickly searched the area within her vision, but she couldn't see anyone.

"No one in there," she whispered.

"Let's try another window," Joe told her.

They softly made their way around the corner of

the house to a window on the side. But when they tried to look inside, their view was blocked by a sturdy wooden shutter.

"On around," Mandie said.

They circled the rest of the house, but the first window was the only one that was not shuttered.

"The fire doesn't give off enough light to see anything in there," Mandie said.

At that precise moment a shot rang out. Mandie heard it ricochet off the tin roof. Just as they heard it an animal let out a nerve-wracking howl.

"A dog!" Mandie said with a loud gasp as she clutched Joe's hand.

"Maybe, but it could be a wild animal. Let's see if we can make our way in that direction," Joe said.

As they stood up, they heard another howl.

"Could it be Samantha?" Mandie whispered as she followed Joe through the bushes in the direction of the sound.

"I'm not sure. I've never heard her howl like that," Joe told her, pushing back the bushes with the butt of his rifle.

Mandie kept listening, but there was no more noise—from the animal or the gun. She was frightened in the dark, but she tried to hide it from Joe.

He paused ahead of her and reached back to hold her hand. He whispered, "Don't be scared."

"Our verse, Joe, let's say our verse," Mandie said, squeezing his hand tightly with her other hand.

Together they recited it, "What time I am afraid, I will trust in Thee."

Mandie straightened up and said, "Now I feel safer. Let's find the source of the howl."

They continued through the woods.

Chapter 6 / Search Continues

The howl Mandie and Joe had heard seemed to have come from the area up the mountain on the other side of the cemetery. As they pushed their way through the thick underbrush, the tall trees obscured any light from the moon that tried peeking through the leaves.

"Aren't you going to whistle for Samantha?" Mandie whispered as she stayed close to Joe in the darkness.

"No," Joe whispered back. "Because we don't want whoever was shooting to know where we are."

Mandie realized that made sense, but she wondered how Joe was going to locate what had made the howling sound? After all, they had not heard it again, so how did Joe know which direction to go? Her questions were cut short by a sudden howl so close that it seemed to come from directly in front of them.

"Wait!" Joe quickly whispered as he touched

her arm to stop her from going on. He grasped her hand.

Mandie felt a quiver run over her body as she took a deep breath and whispered into Joe's ear, "What is that?"

Joe bent to reply in a low whisper, "Sh-h-h-h!"

At the same time, Mandie could hear twigs breaking as something, a man or an animal, moved in the bushes nearby. She held her breath.

"Here!" Joe whispered, quickly stepping to his left and jerking her along.

Mandie stumbled but managed to stay on her feet as Joe pulled her behind a tall oak tree. Her ears strained to listen for more movement, but she couldn't hear a sound. Her heart thumped rapidly in her chest as she stood frozen in her tracks. *Who— or what—was moving through the woods?* she wondered. She was hoping it had not heard her and Joe's movements and stopped to investigate.

The two stood in the darkness so long, Mandie's feet felt numb. She was afraid to even wriggle a toe. And Joe was still squeezing her hand in his. She was about to protest when the howling sound came again, this time from way up the mountainside.

Joe blew out his breath and said softly, "Let's try to follow and see what it is."

"Let's don't get too close to it," Mandie told him as he pushed back the bushes and they moved slowly forward.

"I only want to get close enough to get a look at it," Joe whispered.

They had not gone very far when they suddenly came out onto a narrow trail.

"Well!" Joe exclaimed softly as he looked around. "I never knew this path was here."

"Neither did I," Mandie said. "And it seems to go both ways, downward and upward."

"I believe whatever we've been hearing went upward," Joe whispered. "Come on." He took her hand and they moved quickly up the pathway. Now and then the moonlight found an opening in the trees to shine down on them. And now and then there was a twitter from a bird protesting their intrusion. Small animals scurried away into the darkness.

Mandie watched the surrounding bushes closely as they made their way up the mountainside. The trail seemed smooth except for a bump or a hole once in a while. It was too dark to see these before she stubbed her toes or dropped her foot suddenly into a hole, but Joe kept a firm grasp on her hand.

They were almost as far up the mountain as the graveyard when the noise once again startled them. It seemed to come from below.

"Stop!" Joe whispered. He paused and held her by the hand.

Mandie drew in her breath and said, "Whatever it is must have passed us as it went down." She trembled at the thought of this.

Joe released her hand and put his arm tightly around her shoulders. "I think we'd better go home," he whispered in her ear.

"But how? Whatever is down below we'll have to pass," she said, feeling fear spread over her body.

"We'll go on up and cross the cemetery," Joe told her. "Don't be afraid. I have my rifle, you know."

Mandie glanced up at the tall boy in the darkness and said, "I'm not afraid." She straightened her shoulders. "Let's go."

Joe gave her a squeeze and led the way through the woods. The trail narrowed and Mandie had to follow close behind him until they finally came to the cemetery.

Mandie gave a sigh of relief as she walked into the light of the moon. A few trees grew here and there, but most of the graveyard was open space and was, therefore, much lighter than where they had been. She glanced ahead at the trail leading down the other side of the mountain and remembered they would be under huge trees going down it.

The two paused in the moonlight, and Mandie looked in the direction of her father's grave. Her heartbeat quickened as she thought about how much he had loved her and how much she had loved him. She could still feel his presence.

Joe put an arm around her and said, "We'd better move on."

"Right," Mandie agreed.

At that moment a loud howl came from the woods behind them. Then they heard a shot, which was followed by a man's voice laughing loudly and hilariously.

Joe immediately pulled Mandie behind a big tree and held her tight.

Mandie looked up at him and whispered, "That howl has been a man all along, hasn't it?"

"Yes, and I'd like to get my hands on him," Joe said angrily. "He has been trying to scare us with the shooting and howls."

"Please, Joe, don't try to find him," Mandie said. "Let's just go home. There's no telling who he is. He might be a wild, dangerous man."

"No, I won't try to find him, not with you here,

and not in the dark," Joe replied. "But if we come back in the daylight and I can leave you in a safe place, I'll track him down."

Mandie pulled at Joe's hand. "Let's hurry, Joe," she urged him. "It's late."

"You're right, Mandie," Joe said as he stepped out from behind the tree. "We'll just ignore him the rest of the way."

But it was hard to ignore the man. He kept shooting and howling and laughing, and he seemed to be moving along behind them as they descended the mountain.

Once on the main road, Mandie looked up at Joe and said, "Let's race to your house." She lifted the hem of her long skirt and tucked it into her waistband as they stood there on the road for a moment. There was no sound from the man.

"I'll race with you, but I won't get ahead of you, no matter what," Joe told her. "Because I want to keep you right with me the rest of the way."

"All right then. Let's just run for it," Mandie said, smiling up at the boy, whose eyes shone in the light of the moon.

Joe ran his long fingers through his unruly brown hair, smiled back at her, and replied, "If you feel up to it, young lady."

They ran together, slowing now and then to catch their breath. They ran until they reached the intersection of the road to the schoolhouse. Then Joe put out his hand, signaling Mandie to halt. She stopped beside him and asked, "What?"

Joe took a deep breath to speak. "I'd like to call Samantha to see if she might hear me," he said, looking around in the bright moonlight.

"Joe, I wish we could find her," Mandie said sadly.

Joe whistled several times and called, "Samantha, here girl! Here! Samantha!" He paused to listen, but there was no sound except the chirping of the crickets in the thick underbrush along the road.

The silence of the night was suddenly broken by the sound of wagon wheels and a horse's hooves coming toward them. Mandie squinted to see through the darkness, and as the sound drew nearer, the moonlight revealed Mr. Tallant in his cart with Miss Abigail seated by his side.

Joe quickly spoke, "Mandie, no busybodying, please."

Mandie stepped over to join him. "Joe!" she exclaimed. "Let's just watch and see where they go."

Mr. Tallant slowed his horse for the turn into the road to the schoolhouse. As he did, he waved and asked, "Still haven't found your dog, Joe?"

"No, sir, not yet," Joe called to him.

"I'm sorry," Mr. Tallant replied, slowing his horse even more. "I've alerted everyone down the road back that way to be on the lookout for her. Let me know if I can be of any help."

Mandie was watching Miss Abigail. She kept her head bent so that the large hat she was wearing hid her face from view. Mr. Tallant completed the turn and drove on down toward the schoolhouse.

"Thank you, sir," Joe called after him.

Mandie looked at Joe as the cart passed out of sight. "Miss Abigail didn't say a word," she said.

"Why should she? She maybe didn't have anything to say," Joe replied.

"Well, she could have at least said hello," Mandie told him. Then she added, "Let's go back down by the schoolhouse to look for Samantha. But let's take the regular road."

Joe looked at her and frowned. "It is late, Mandie, and you know as well as I do that Miss Abigail lives down that way and Mr. Tallant is evidently taking her home. Therefore, you just want to go spy on them," he said.

"Honest, Joe, I don't," Mandie said firmly. "I just have a feeling we ought to look around down there again." She looked him straight in the eyes.

Joe sighed and said, "All right, but we're only going to run around the schoolhouse. We're not taking time to check up on Mr. Tallant and Miss Abigail. Come on. Let's go."

The two walked down the road Mr. Tallant had traveled, and when the school building came into view, Joe began whistling and calling his dog. He listened in between for any sound from Samantha. When they reached the building, they circled the schoolhouse.

Finally Joe said, "Nothing here. Let's go home."

Mandie walked up on the porch of the building and tried the door. It was locked.

"What are you doing?" Joe called to her.

"I was just going to look inside, but the door is locked," she replied as she walked across to the steps. As she lifted her long skirt to step down, she heard a faint *meow* somewhere nearby. She quickly stood still and listened.

"Now what?" Joe asked as he watched her.

"I hear something. Be quiet a minute," Mandie said as she heard the meow again.

It was coming from inside the schoolhouse. *There must be a cat in there,* she thought. Joe joined her on the porch and she could tell he was hearing it, too.

"A cat," Joe said.

"Yes, a cat. And it's locked inside," Mandie told him.

"It's probably Mr. Tallant's cat or it wouldn't be locked up inside the schoolhouse. Come on. Let's go," Joe insisted.

Mandie tried to see through the window, but the shutter was closed. The cat meowed again, and this time Mandie exclaimed with certainty, "It's Snowball! I know his meow! And he's locked inside!"

"Snowball is in your room back at my house, remember?" Joe told her.

"I know he *was*, but Snowball is a smart cat, and somehow he got out and came here," Mandie said. Then she began calling, "Snowball, Snowball! Kitty, kitty!" She stood close to the door.

A loud meowing began on the other side. Evidently the cat had come up to the door. Mandie shook the door, trying to open it even though she knew it was locked.

"Snowball! How did you get in there?" Mandie yelled at him.

Joe stepped up on the porch and came to her side. "Mandie, you can't be sure that's your cat in there," he said.

"Yes I can," she argued. "I know Snowball's meow just like you know your dog's bark."

"Well, I don't know how you're going to get him out," Joe replied.

"We can go down to Miss Abigail's house and ask Mr. Tallant to unlock the door," Mandie said as she looked up at him.

"Go to Miss Abigail's?" Joe asked. "Why, she

would think we're just snooping, because she knows we saw her with Mr. Tallant."

"If you don't want to go, then I'll go by myself, but I'm going to get Snowball out of here some way," Mandie said as she started down the steps.

"Wait," Joe said, following her. "I'll go with you if you're deadbent on going."

They hurried around to the road behind the schoolhouse and came to the smaller road leading to Miss Abigail's house. Mandie looked ahead as they walked, but it was too dark to see Miss Abigail's house until they were almost in front of it. The two-story structure was covered with weatherboarding painted white, and was probably the most expensive dwelling in the area—according to gossip Mandie remembered hearing when she was living with her father. All the local women pondered the fact that, even with a house like this, Miss Abigail had never been able to get herself a husband.

"I see Mr. Tallant's cart over there," Joe said, pointing to the driveway that ran down to the barn. "So he's still here."

Mandie looked and saw that the horse was still harnessed to the cart. Therefore, Mr. Tallant was probably not planning to stay long. "Thank goodness," she said as they continued on up to the long, wide veranda on the front of the house.

"Well, come sit awhile," Mr. Tallant said as he rose from a chair behind the climbing rose covering the trellis in front of the porch.

"Oh, Mr. Tallant, I'm sorry to bother you, but my cat, Snowball, is locked up in your schoolhouse," Mandie said as she and Joe walked down the porch toward the schoolmaster.

"Cat? Locked up in the schoolhouse?" Mr. Tallant questioned.

"Yes, sir," Joe replied. "You see, we went there looking for Samantha. Mandie heard a cat meowing inside and decided it was Snowball."

"Sit down, Mandie, Joe," Miss Abigail invited, standing up in a dark corner from a chair near Mr. Tallant's.

"Thank you, Miss Abigail, but we don't really have time. If Mr. Tallant would please unlock the schoolhouse so I can get my cat, I'd appreciate it," Mandie replied as she looked up at the tall woman.

"I'll be glad to, but I can't imagine how a cat could have been locked inside," Mr. Tallant said. Looking at Miss Abigail, he said, "This will only take a few minutes. We'll walk up to the schoolhouse and I'll be back shortly for my cart."

"Of course," Miss Abigail said. "I'll be right here." Turning to the two young people she added, "Y'all do come back to visit sometime."

"Yes, ma'am, thank you," Mandie said, following Mr. Tallant down the porch.

"Thank you, Miss Abigail," Joe called back as he caught up with Mandie.

As the three hurried the short distance to the schoolhouse, Mandie tried to explain. "You see, Snowball was shut up in my room at Joe's house, but somehow he was able to get out. And for some reason he came here to the schoolhouse."

"If the cat inside even *is* Snowball," Joe added.

"Joe, I said I'm sure it's Snowball," Mandie insisted as they entered the yard of the building.

"Never mind what cat it is, it shouldn't be inside the schoolhouse," Mr. Tallant told them as he stepped up on the front porch, inserted a large key in the huge keyhole, and pushed the door open. "I didn't see any cat when I locked the door a while ago. I came in to get some papers to discuss with Miss Abigail."

The cat rushed out, and Mandie nearly stumbled over him. She looked down and saw immediately that it was Snowball. She picked him up to look into his blue eyes and asked, "Snowball, how in this world did you get locked up inside the schoolhouse?"

"Well, that settles that," Mr. Tallant said as he locked the door.

"Oh, thank you, Mr. Tallant," Mandie said. "If I had gone on back to Joe's house and found Snowball missing, then I would have had to go out and look for him, like Joe is doing for Samantha."

"That is strange about your dog being missing," the schoolmaster told Joe as they left the porch.

"Yes, sir, and I have to keep on looking until I do find her," Joe replied.

"Can I give you two a ride home?" Mr. Tallant asked Joe.

"No, thank you. We'll just walk. It isn't far, you know, and I'll keep on looking for Samantha on the way," Joe said.

"Good-night then. I hope you find Samantha soon," Mr. Tallant said as he walked around to the back of the schoolhouse on his way to Miss Abigail's.

"Thanks," Joe called as they went on toward the main road.

Mandie noticed Snowball didn't have his leash on. She had removed it when she shut him up in her room. She figured that no one had let him out, at least not on purpose.

Mandie looked up at Joe as they walked along. "Snowball must have come into the schoolhouse while Mr. Tallant was there," she said. "And he didn't see him, so he locked the door and left."

"I suppose," Joe said. "That cat sure gets around."

"I can't imagine how he got out of your house," Mandie said. She held Snowball tightly in her arms. And then she quickly changed the subject. "Did you notice they were sitting in the dark on the porch? There was plenty of moonlight on the rest of the porch, but they were sitting behind the rose trellis."

"What difference does it make *where* they were sitting?" Joe asked. "It's none of our business!"

"Oh, Joe, don't be an old stick-in-the-mud," Mandie told him as she looked up and smiled. "There may be a romance going between them."

Joe stopped and looked down at her. "Romance?" he asked. "That doesn't concern us." He straightened up to his full height as he walked and said, "Come on. I'll race you the rest of the way."

Mandie held Snowball with one arm and tucked the hem of her skirt into the waistband with the other hand. "I'm ready," she said. "Let's go."

They ran the short distance to Joe's house, and the whole time Mandie was wondering how her cat had managed to get out of the house and, of all things, why he'd gone to the schoolhouse.

Chapter 7 / Was It a Dream?

When Mandie and Joe arrived at his house, he led the way around to the back. "I want to look and see if Samantha is in the barn, and I should also put my rifle up," he said. "And since you have Snowball, I'll just meet you inside in a few minutes."

"All right," Mandie agreed. "I'll put Snowball in my room and see where your mother is."

When Mandie came in through the back door of the house, she found Mrs. Woodard sitting by a lamp at one end of the kitchen. She was embroidering the pillowcases. She looked up at Mandie and said, "Oh, thank goodness you caught that cat."

"He was locked inside the schoolhouse, and it just happened that Mr. Tallant was taking Miss Abigail home and passed us, so we got him to unlock the door," Mandie tried to explain as she set the cat down at a bowl of water set out for him near the iron cookstove. She sat down in a chair nearby.

Mrs. Woodard quickly looked up. "Mr. Tallant

was taking Miss Abigail home?" she asked.

"Yes, ma'am," Mandie replied with a smile. "You see, they had just passed us on the road. They were in his cart."

"My, my!" Mrs. Woodard said with a big smile. "I wonder if something is going on between the two of them."

"We went down to Miss Abigail's house to get him, and they were sitting on the front porch in the dark behind the rose trellis," Mandie explained, still smiling.

"You don't say!" Mrs. Woodard exclaimed. "And did he go back to Miss Abigail's house after he let y'all into the schoolhouse?"

"Yes, ma'am. He said he had to go back and get his cart, he said," Mandie told her.

Joe came into the kitchen and overheard the last remark. He looked impatiently from her to his mother.

"Miss Abigail must be coming out of her shell after all these years mourning over her dead sweetheart," Mrs. Woodard said with a little laugh.

"Mama!" Joe exclaimed. "You're not joining in this romance business with Mandie, are you?"

Mrs. Woodard looked at him and laughed. "You men are all just alike. You never understand how important a little romance is to a woman."

Joe shrugged and changed the subject. "Dad's horse and buggy aren't in the barn. Isn't he back yet?" he asked.

"No, he hasn't returned yet," Mrs. Woodard said. "You know it's a long way over there to the Guytons'. Not only that, the road is rough, so I'll look for him when I see him. And you haven't found Samantha, have you?"

"No, ma'am," Joe replied. "But at least Mandie found Snowball." He sat down near them.

"I'm glad, because I was afraid he was going to be lost for good and Amanda would think I let him out," Mrs. Woodard said.

Mandie quickly looked at her and asked, "How did he get out of my room?"

"This is hard to believe," Mrs. Woodard said. "I was out in the yard beneath the window to your room, dear, and I heard a loud meow. I looked around and finally spotted Snowball sitting on a limb on that big chestnut tree that grows up by your room upstairs."

Mandie gasped. "How did he get up there?" she asked.

"The window was open, and the limbs grow close to the house," Mrs. Woodard continued. "I figured he came out through the window into the tree. And you know, he wouldn't come down for anything. He just sat there and cried."

"How did he get down?" Joe asked.

"Well, I have to confess," Mrs. Woodard said, "I threw a small rock to hit the limb next to him, just trying to get him to move. Of course the rock missed him, but he did move in such a hurry that he fell down a couple of limbs and sat there crying again. The branch he was on was not big enough to support him, so it bent and he came falling and sliding down the tree."

"He didn't get hurt, did he?" Mandie quickly asked as she glanced at the white cat now curled up asleep by the cookstove.

"No, he caught some branches as he came down and, when he landed on the ground, he took off running. I couldn't very well go after him in the dark with no one else here. Thank goodness you found him," Mrs. Woodard explained.

"Yes, thank goodness I found him," Mandie agreed.

"The puppies look all right," Joe remarked.

"Yes, they've learned to lap up the milk I give them. They seem to be doing all right," Mrs. Woodard said. "But I sure wish you could find Samantha."

"So do I," Joe agreed with a worried expression on his face. He stood up and looked over at the cookstove. "Anything to eat?"

Mrs. Woodard rose from her chair and laid down the pillowcase. "Of course," she said. "I knew you two would be hungry when you got back." She walked over to the stove and opened the warmer. "These biscuits are still warm, and we've got molasses and butter to go on them."

"Sounds good," Mandie said.

Mrs. Woodard pulled a small pan of biscuits out and turned to look at Joe. "Now if you'll run out to the springhouse and bring in a jug of sweet milk, I'll get the molasses and butter out of the larder." She set the pan on top of the stove.

"Be right back," Joe said, quickly leaving the room.

"Can I help?" Mandie asked as Mrs. Woodard went toward the end of the room to the larder, where the food supplies were kept.

"Get some glasses and plates down from the cupboard if you will, dear," Mrs. Woodard said as she opened the door to the larder.

By the time Joe returned with the milk, everything was ready on the long table. Mrs. Woodard filled the glasses and they sat down at one end.

As she buttered the biscuits, Mrs. Woodard asked, "And did y'all go by your father's house, Amanda?"

"Yes, ma'am," Mandie replied, accepting a biscuit and pouring a little molasses on it from the small jug. "There wasn't a light in the house, but one of the shutters was open, and we could see light from the fireplace. So somebody must have been in there to have a fire in the fireplace."

Joe took the jug and spread molasses on his biscuit. "We heard this howling sound and tried to track it down in case it might be Samantha, but it turned out to be some wild man who was howling and shooting and laughing all over the mountain," he replied.

"A wild man?" Mrs. Woodard questioned. "Who could it have been?" She began eating her biscuit.

"I have no idea," Joe said.

"We're so far back in the mountains that strangers very seldom come here," Mrs. Woodard said. "I wonder if it could have been someone we know."

"We never did get to see him," Mandie explained. "He just followed us all over the mountain without coming out where we could tell who he was."

"You don't think he was trying to harm y'all?" Mrs. Woodard asked Joe.

"No, ma'am," he said as he swallowed a mouthful of biscuit. "I'm sure he just wanted to scare us for some reason."

"He probably thought he could scare us enough that we would go away, which we did," Mandie said, licking the molasses dripping from her biscuit.

"That's strange," Mrs. Woodard said. She looked at Mandie and asked, "And what do you intend to do about your father's house?"

"I just don't know," Mandie replied. "I'm sure someone is in it, but it may be someone just camping out there, because no one is farming the land and there's no livestock—not even a chicken."

"Maybe we should ask the sheriff to look into it," Mrs. Woodard suggested.

"Mama, there's nothing he can do," Joe said. "If we can't get whoever it is to come to the door, neither can the sheriff. And he certainly won't break the door down to get inside."

"I suppose you're right," Mrs. Woodard agreed.

Snowball had come over to the table and was rubbing around Mandie's ankles. Mandie bent to look at him. "I knew you wouldn't sleep long if you smelled food," she said.

Mrs. Woodard got up and went to the stove. "Here, I saved him the meat scraps from supper, but he ran away before I could give them to him," she said as she took a covered dish and dumped the contents into his bowl on the floor.

Snowball came running and immediately began devouring the food.

"I need you to look at that window in Amanda's room, Joe," Mrs. Woodard said as she sat back down at the table. "It's stuck, and I can't get it closed."

"I'll get it shut. We don't want that cat going out anymore," Joe said, giving Mandie a smile.

"No, because he could get killed falling from that tree," Mandie agreed. "I'll take him with me when we go back out tomorrow."

"Do you think you can hold on to him?" Joe asked.

Before she could answer, Mrs. Woodard said, "If Joe can't get that window closed, we'll just put him in another room upstairs while you're gone."

"Thank you, Mrs. Woodard, but he needs some exercise and fresh air, so I'll take him with me," Mandie said, drinking the last of the milk in her glass.

When they had all finished, Mandie and Joe

cleared the table. Mrs. Woodard told them, "Now y'all just run along. I'll finish up. I'm going to be working on that pillowcase for a while longer. And maybe your father will come in before I retire for the night."

"I suppose I am a little sleepy," Mandie said. "Good-night, Mrs. Woodard." She picked up Snowball and turned to leave the kitchen.

"Good-night, Mama," Joe replied as he left the room with Mandie and Snowball.

When they got to Mandie's room Joe worked on the window, trying to force it down. As Mandie watched, it came down to within two inches of the sill and refused to go any farther.

"It just won't go all the way," Joe said, beating at the window frame with his hands.

"That's all right, Joe," Mandie said. "Snowball can't get out an opening that narrow. Thanks. I'll see you at breakfast in the morning."

Joe looked at the partly open window and shrugged his shoulders. "I don't think Snowball can get out," he said. "At least I hope not." He went to the door and added, "Good-night. See you bright and early."

"Good-night," Mandie replied as she closed the door behind him.

Snowball had already curled up on the foot of the bed as she began undressing for the night. The night air had become chilly, so she pulled a heavy quilt up over her when she slid in between the sheets.

Mandie was tired, worn out with all the searching they had been doing, so she soon fell asleep. She was dreaming of her father when something brought her wide awake.

She instantly sat up in bed. Talking to herself, she asked, "What was that noise that woke me up?"

She looked over at the window in the moonlight, and it was still in the same position. Snowball woke up and began stretching.

Her heart was beating fast and she felt frightened, but she didn't understand why. She thought about it for a while and she listened, but couldn't hear a thing. Finally she lay down to go back to sleep.

She was dozing when she suddenly heard the howling sound they had heard on the mountain. Then came the same laugh. She sat straight up in bed again and pulled the quilt around her. Holding her breath, she waited and waited to see if it would be repeated, but there was only silence.

"That man on the mountain must have followed us home," she exclaimed to herself. "I wonder if Joe heard it."

She hoped Dr. Woodard had come home by now. Sleep finally overcame her again and she curled up under the cover. Snowball moved up to sleep on the other pillow. She drifted off thinking she had maybe only imagined the noise.

———

The next thing Mandie knew, Snowball was purring in her face, and she sat up to see the sun rising over the distant hill. She jumped out of bed, stretched, and began dressing.

When she was ready to go downstairs, she suddenly remembered waking up during the night. She sat down on the edge of the bed she had just made up and thought about it for a moment.

"Did I imagine I heard that wild man, or was it real?" she asked herself. "If I go downstairs and tell everybody about it, they may think it was all a dream. But then, maybe I was dreaming."

Snowball jumped up on the bed behind her and began rubbing against her back. She reached back to pat his head.

"Oh, what should I do?" she asked herself as she stood up. She did some more thinking and then decided. "If I tell them and they think it was a dream, I don't suppose it will really matter. But I do think it was real—I did hear that wild man. But how in the world did he get here and where is he now?"

She shivered as she thought about the possibility of the man being near the house. Who was he? And exactly what did he want?

At that moment Joe tapped on her door and called, "Good morning. Are you ready for breakfast yet?"

Mandie rushed across the room and opened the door. Making sure Snowball didn't get out of the room, she closed it and joined Joe in the hallway.

"Good morning," she greeted him. "I should have already gone downstairs to help your mother with breakfast." She could smell the bacon frying as they walked down the stairs.

"You're wrong there," Joe said. "On nights when my father is away until late and she sits up waiting for him, my mother always has Mrs. Miller come in and fix breakfast for me so she can sleep late. Of course I could always cook for myself, but Mama says it gives Mrs. Miller an opportunity to make a little extra money."

"Then that's Mrs. Miller cooking that good-smelling bacon," Mandie said with a big smile as they walked through the downstairs hallway toward the kitchen.

"And eggs, and biscuits, and grits, of course, and sometimes sweet rolls, and who knows what else.

Mrs. Miller is a delicious cook," Joe said, laughing.

Mandie also laughed as she said, "A delicious cook? I never heard of such a person."

Joe pushed open the door to the kitchen and they went in. Mrs. Miller greeted them with a smile as she said, "Good morning. You're right on the dot. Everything is ready."

The young people returned the greeting.

She was standing by the stove, which held various pots and pans. The table was set for two, and Mandie asked, "Only two plates?"

"Yes, dear, only you and Joe," Mrs. Miller replied.

As they stood by the table, Joe asked, "Aren't you eating with us?"

"Oh no, not this morning. As soon as I get the food on the table for y'all, I have to run home and feed my husband. I'll eat with him," Mrs. Miller explained. "Now let me get this stuff over there for you. Y'all just sit down now and, Joe, I placed the coffeepot so you can pour it."

The two young people sat down. Joe poured the coffee and Mrs. Miller began bringing bowls and platters to the table. Mandie understood what Joe had meant when he said 'who knows what else,' because there were even fried pork chops and sweet rolls, which smelled so delicious she could hardly wait to bite into one.

"It all looks so mouth-watering," Mandie remarked as she helped herself to the various dishes.

"You'd better eat fast, because I'm starving," Joe joked as he filled his plate.

Mrs. Miller stood back and smiled at them. "Now when y'all finish eating, just leave everything where it is," she said. "I'll be back and have it all cleaned up and more ready for the doctor and Mrs. Woodard before they come downstairs." She untied her apron and hung it on a hook near the stove.

"Thanks, Mrs. Miller," Mandie said with her mouth full of egg. "Everything is absolutely delicious."

"Amen," Joe added.

"Bye now," she said, going out the back door.

As she ate, Mandie thought about the noise the night before, and she finally decided to mention it to Joe.

As she sipped her coffee, she said, "Did you hear anything during the night?"

Joe looked at her in surprise and asked, "No, why?"

"Something woke me up last night," Mandie began, watching for his reaction.

"Something woke you up? What was it?" Joe asked as he hungrily ate his pork chop.

"I'm not positive, but I believe it was the same noise we heard on the mountain—that man howling and laughing," Mandie explained as she kept looking at Joe.

"That man?" Joe asked as he laid down his fork and knife. "All the way over here to our house? Are you sure?"

"No, Joe, I'm not sure," Mandie replied, setting down her coffee cup and straightening up in her chair. "But something woke me, and at that time I thought I heard the man. I might be wrong, but I don't think it was a dream either."

"I suppose it's possible he could have followed us home last night," Joe said. "Or he might have known who we were. But why was he doing all this crazy stuff? Did you hear this noise all during the night?"

"No, I only heard it once," Mandie said. "It puzzles me, too."

"Did you hear any shooting?" Joe asked.

Mandie thought about that for a second. "No, I don't think so," she said. "Just the laughing after that terrible howling."

"I need to look around outside," Joe said. "As soon as I finish. I'll get my rifle just in case."

"Is your father home yet?" Mandie asked.

"I'm not sure," Joe said. "But I'll look to see whether his horse and buggy are in the barn. Then I'll know."

"I'll go with you," Mandie said. "First I just need to run up with some scraps for Snowball's breakfast and be sure he's still in the room."

"You ought to wait until I look around before you come outside," Joe said.

Mandie looked at him and said, "Joe, you know you can't keep me in the house when something is going on. Besides, if you do run into the wild man or someone strange you might need some help."

She stood up and quickly gathered food scraps for her cat.

"Wait for me," she told Joe as she left the room. He was still drinking his coffee.

She wanted to see for herself if Joe discovered someone on their property. Then she remembered Mrs. Miller had come to the house and had gone back to hers. She had not mentioned seeing any stranger.

Maybe it was a dream, or maybe the man is already gone, she thought.

Chapter 8 / Accused!

Mandie gave Snowball his breakfast in her room and checked the water bowl to be sure it was full. Then telling him to behave, she hurried downstairs to join Joe, who was waiting in the kitchen. "I'm ready," Mandie told him as she entered the room.

"I need to get my rifle," Joe said as he stood up.

"You know I've been wondering about where you actually keep your rifle," Mandie said. "I know one time you got it from the barn, but I think you had left it on the back porch another time. How do you keep up with it?"

"We have other guns in the house," Joe explained. "In the hall closet, to be exact. I mostly carry my rifle around wherever I think I might need it. If I leave it in the barn it comes in handy if some wild animal attacks any of our stock, and if it's on the back porch it's convenient to get when I'm going hunting through the woods." He led the way to the back door and opened it.

"So where did you leave it this time?" Mandie asked as they went out onto the back porch.

Joe looked at her and grinned. "In the shed between here and the barn," he said. "I couldn't decide where I might need it next when we came home last night. And right now we'd better keep an eye out for any strangers in the yard until I get to the shed."

Mandie looked all around as they hurried toward the small shed, and Joe watched ahead. Once Joe had retrieved his rifle, the two began moving across the yard and searching behind bushes and trees. They worked their way down to the barn without finding anyone.

"Look! Your father's buggy is in the barn," Mandie said as the entrance of the building came into view.

"Yes, I'm glad he's back," Joe said as they walked on toward the building.

"Could we stop and see the puppies?" Mandie asked as they entered the barn.

"Sure," Joe said, stopping by a stall to rub the head of his father's horse. The big animal nickered, and Joe gave him a piece of sugar from a bag nearby. The horse quickly swallowed it and began rubbing his head against Joe's hand.

"He acts just like Snowball when he wants to thank me. He rubs my hand with his head," Mandie remarked as she watched.

"I'm afraid he's spoiled rotten by my father. He's always getting goodies," Joe said as they walked on down to the stall where the small animals were living.

Mandie followed and she eagerly bent over the railing to watch the little puppies shoving and jostling each other as they whined and fussed.

"They are so adorable," she exclaimed.

"They seem to be all right, Joe said. "I'll leave it to my mother to give them milk. She enjoys tending to little animals." He turned to leave.

"What are we going to do today?" Mandie asked as they walked back outside.

"I don't really know," Joe said. "Let's sit down over here." He indicated a bench made of tough planks supported by sawed-off tree trunks.

As they sat down he continued, "I don't think anyone is on our property, at least not anywhere near the house." He looked at her and asked, "Do you think you really heard the man, or do you think it was on your mind and you dreamed about him?"

Mandie hesitated. "We-e-e-ll," she said, dragging out the word, "I'm pretty sure I actually heard him." She shrugged and added, "But then maybe it was a dream. I don't suppose it makes any difference now, since we haven't found anyone around here."

"But we should still keep watch for any strangers," Joe told her.

"Right," Mandie agreed, then she remembered Snowball. "I need to take Snowball out for a walk. Would you want to just stroll down the road a piece, nowhere in particular?"

Joe looked at her and asked, "Nowhere in particular? You don't want to go back to your father's house in hopes of seeing someone there?"

"Well, I suppose we could, but remember that wild man may see us and start all that howling and shooting and laughing," Mandie replied.

"I'll have my rifle, and as long as he doesn't physically bother us, then we can just ignore him. That might be the best way to get rid of him anyway," Joe said.

Mandie looked at him and asked, "You don't think he's dangerous?"

"Probably not, at least not as long as we don't bother him," Joe said.

"All right, I'll run up and get Snowball," Mandie said as she stood up.

"I'll wait here," Joe said.

At that moment Mrs. Miller came up the pathway that led to her house. She was hurrying and, when she saw the two young people, she said, "I hope I wasn't gone too long."

"Oh no, ma'am," Joe said as he, too, stood up.

"Mrs. Miller, did you see a stranger on the Woodards' property this morning?" Mandie asked. "A man?"

"A strange man?" Mrs. Miller questioned. She frowned and said, "No, I haven't seen anyone at all. Were y'all looking for someone?"

"Not really," Joe said. "We just thought a stranger might have walked across the yard last night after we went to bed."

"Oh goodness!" Mrs. Miller exclaimed. "Is something missing?"

"Not that I know of," Joe replied.

"It's a man from over on the mountain who we're talking about," Mandie explained.

"Is he dangerous?" the woman asked.

"We don't think so. I believe he just wants to annoy people," Joe said. "Anyway, don't worry about it. Mandie and I are the ones he's trying to irritate. Just keep watch as you go back and forth."

"Well, let me hurry and get breakfast for your mama and daddy," she said. "I can take care of myself." She suddenly pulled a sharp knife out of the pocket of her full skirt and held it up. "This is my protection. I carry it everywhere I go. Now you two be careful."

"Yes, ma'am," the two chorused as they looked at each other, and Mrs. Miller walked on toward the house.

"Well!" Joe exclaimed. "I didn't realize she carried a knife!"

"Good for her," Mandie said with a smile. "Now I'll go get Snowball. Be right back."

She hurried to the house and, as she went through the kitchen, she didn't see anyone but Mrs. Miller, who was busily stacking dirty dishes. Evidently Dr. and Mrs. Woodard were still sleeping.

She ran up the stairs to her room and opened the door to find Snowball pawing at the window where it was open.

"We fixed you, Snowball," Mandie told him as she reached to pick him up. "You can't get through that small opening, and there's no way you can open the window."

She reached for his red leash, which lay on the bureau, and quickly snapped it onto his red collar.

"We're going for a walk, and you had better behave," Mandie told him as she gathered up the leash and the white cat and rushed back downstairs to the kitchen.

"We're going for a walk with my cat," Mandie said when Mrs. Miller paused in her work at the sink. "Just in the direction of the schoolhouse, I suppose. We won't be gone long. If you would let Dr. and Mrs. Woodard know, I'd appreciate it."

"Oh, sure I will," Mrs. Miller said. "Just you two be careful and be back at noon for dinner."

"Thank you, Mrs. Miller," Mandie said as she left

through the back door and raced across the yard to join Joe.

He saw her coming and came up the path to meet her.

"Which way do you want to go?" Joe asked as they started down the driveway toward the road.

"It doesn't matter, but I suppose the usual way. We always head toward my father's house," she replied as Snowball squirmed to get down.

"Fine," Joe said. He patted the pocket in his pants. "I went and got a couple of extra shells."

"That's good, but I hope you won't need to use your rifle," Mandie said as they reached the road. She stooped to set Snowball down at the end of his leash and kept a firm hold on it. "Now you can walk, but you'd better not run away, Snowball."

Snowball looked up at his mistress and meowed, then he pulled at the leash as he tried to walk on.

Joe laughed and said, "You don't think that cat really understands what you say, do you?"

Mandie held the end of the leash. "I really believe he can understand some things I say," she said. "He's a smart cat."

"I hear you," Joe joked.

They strolled down the road with Snowball straining against his leash most of the time. Mandie noticed that Joe kept watching the fields along the way, but he didn't stop to call Samantha.

Finally she asked, "Aren't you even going to whistle for Samantha? You never know when she might hear you."

"I suppose so," Joe said sadly. He stopped and whistled. He called, "Samantha!" but received no response.

"You know, Joe, you have a problem—Samantha is missing. And I have a problem—someone is in my father's house and won't come to the door. Do you think the problems could be related?" Mandie asked.

"And don't forget the problem with the wild man," Joe reminded her. "Yes, it could all be connected somehow."

"And don't forget that Mr. Tallant and Miss Abigail," Mandie added with a smile.

"They are not our problem, Mandie," Joe said. "I wish you would forget about them."

"Oh, Joe, I can't forget about them. I'm hoping they'll get married," she replied as Snowball pulled her forward with his leash.

"Mandie, you don't know whether they even love each other or not, and here you're hoping they'll get married," Joe protested.

"I'm guessing they're in love," Mandie replied with a smirk. "Else why would they be seeing each other?"

"There are other reasons for two adults to see each other, you know," Joe said. "Maybe it's business between them."

"Would they do business sitting on her front porch in the dark behind the rose trellis?" Mandie asked with a smile. She switched the end of the leash to her other hand. Snowball picked this opportunity to escape. He managed to jerk the leash out of her hand and go flying down the road.

"Snowball! Come back here!" Mandie cried, lifting her long skirt and running after him.

Joe followed her, and they tried to pin Snowball between the two of them, but the white cat took a shortcut across a field to get onto the road to the schoolhouse.

Mandie kept calling him and running across the rough field. When Snowball was out of sight, Joe came toward her and said, "Let's get on the road. This is too slow."

Mandie nodded and followed him onto the hard packed dirt road. This was smoother and she could run faster. Joe's long legs got ahead of her and he yelled back, "I see him! He's going inside the schoolhouse!"

Mandie wondered how Snowball could get into the schoolhouse. *Is the door open?* she wondered. She finally caught up with Joe as he waited at the steps of the building.

"You don't have to hurry," said Joe as he tried to catch his breath. "He went inside. I saw him."

Mandie swallowed hard to control her heavy breathing. "Let's see what he's doing in there," she said as she walked toward the slightly open door. "If we go inside and close the door he can't get out."

Joe leaned his rifle against the post. He followed Mandie and they pushed the door shut behind them as they looked around the schoolroom. Snowball was sitting on a shelf in the middle of Mr. Tallant's papers, washing his face.

"Oh, Snowball, I could spank you good," Mandie said as she approached the cat. Joe stood watching.

But Snowball was too quick for her. He jumped down from the shelf and led her on a chase around the room. He tried to jump onto the shelf under the blackboard, but the space was too small for him and he tumbled onto the floor.

As Mandie grabbed for him she noticed writing on the blackboard. She gasped when she read it. "Look! Someone has written on the blackboard again," she exclaimed.

"I saw it the same time you did," Joe said as he stared at the scribbling.

"And see what it says—'Miss Abigail loves Mr. Tallant.' " She quickly looked at Joe and said, "And I didn't write that!"

Joe picked up the eraser and said, "Well, whoever wrote it will be disappointed to know I have erased it."

"Joe, don't! We need to find out what's going on," Mandie begged.

At that moment the door opened, and Mandie and Joe both glanced back to see Mr. Tallant as he came into the room.

Mandie and Joe froze as the man read the writing on the blackboard. "Well, now I'm disappointed in you two to write such untruths on my blackboard," he said, standing before them.

"We didn't write that, Mr. Tallant," Mandie argued. "In fact, Joe was just about to erase it when you came in."

"That's right, sir," Joe said. "I would never do such a thing."

Mr. Tallant looked at the two of them sternly and said, "I'm sorry, but I'm not sure I believe your story. How did you get in here?"

"The door was open," Mandie replied as she watched Snowball prowling around. She held her breath, hoping he wouldn't get into anything.

"And Mandie's cat got away from us out on the road and ran down here. The door was open, so Snowball just came inside and we came after him," Joe tried to explain.

Mandie thought Mr. Tallant looked doubtful. She desperately tried to think of something to say that would persuade him to believe them. Then she remembered Snowball being locked in the school.

"Someone must have another key, Mr. Tallant, because if you remember, Snowball was locked in here last night, and you said you had locked the door, and we never did figure out how he got inside," Mandie explained.

Mr. Tallant frowned and said, "The only other key I know of is at your father's house, and it is kept there for emergencies, Joe. Therefore, it would be very easy for you two to use the other key."

Mandie and Joe looked at each other in surprise.

"I never knew my father had an extra key to the schoolhouse, Mr. Tallant," Joe argued. "And I'm sure it must be kept in a safe place."

"Mr. Tallant, we did not unlock the door to this schoolhouse, not this morning nor yesterday, nor any other time," Mandie said emphatically, stomping her foot. "You can believe what you like, but we are not guilty."

"And you can check with my father about the other key. He's at home this morning," Joe added.

Mr. Tallant frowned, shook his head, and silently reached for the eraser. He wiped the writing off the blackboard.

Mandie, figuring she and Joe were already in trouble, couldn't resist asking, "Joe told me someone wrote on the blackboard before, and that you found it and erased it before anyone else saw it, and that's why you keep the door locked now. Couldn't this have been written by the same person who did that? And I wasn't even here when that other writing happened."

Mr. Tallant thought for a moment, then looked at Joe and said, "But Joe was here."

"Just stop and think a moment. Do you really

believe I would do such a thing?'' Joe asked. "Surely you don't think I wrote whatever it was you found before on the blackboard, or this either. You told the class you found it, erased it, and had an idea as to who had done it. Were you thinking then that I had done it, Mr. Tallant?"

Mr. Tallant cleared his throat, walked across the room, and sat down behind his desk. "I think you two had better leave now. And I will discuss this with your father, Joe. Now get out and don't let me catch you in here again."

Mandie and Joe looked at each other in surprise. She ran to pick up Snowball, and as she and Joe started out the door, he turned back and said, "I'm sorry you feel like this about such a thing, Mr. Tallant.''

The schoolmaster didn't reply, but kept busy shuffling papers around on his desk until the two had closed the door behind them.

On the porch, Mandie drew in a deep breath and said, "He sure acted strange. He just couldn't see anything but his own way."

Joe picked up his rifle and said, "That's because the message was so personal to him."

"Let's walk down the back road, Joe," Mandie suggested as she started around the schoolhouse. She held on to Snowball.

"All right," Joe agreed.

Mandie could tell he was really upset with the whole matter. And she didn't blame him. Mr. Tallant should have known Joe well enough to realize he would never do such a foolish thing.

Joe glanced at her as though he could read her thoughts and said, "Don't let it bother you. I will discuss it with my father as soon as I get home. I'm sure he will talk to Mr. Tallant about it."

"I hope so," Mandie replied. "Snowball, quit squirming. You're not going to get down. I don't want to have to chase you again."

As they walked on down the back road, around the curve where the lanes branched off to Nimrod's house and Miss Abigail's house, Snowball began acting strange. He hissed and growled.

Mandie and Joe both looked at him.

"What's wrong with him?" asked Joe. "I've never seen him act so angry before."

"I don't know, but I do know he's going to catch it if he scratches me," Mandie said. Then she added, "Maybe he wants down to find a sandbox." She set him down at the end of the leash, but kept it wrapped around her wrist.

"He's just trying to run away again," Joe said, watching the cat.

"I think you're right," Mandie said, and picked him back up. "Let's hurry and get on the main road. I can let him walk there, and if he tries to run away, I can catch him better."

Joe laughed and said, "The main road is where he managed to get away from you, remember?"

"Oh well, I can walk better on the main road," Mandie said.

They cut across fields to get back onto the main road in the direction of her father's house. Mandie set Snowball down, and he walked ahead of them at the end of his leash without any more trouble. Mandie wondered what could have been in the bushes on that road that he wanted to investigate. She thought it was probably just a rabbit or a squirrel.

Chapter 9 / Measles!

Mandie and Joe walked on toward her father's house. Snowball tried to get away, pulling at the end of the leash, so Mandie carried him part of the time.

"I would say that Mr. Tallant is in love with Miss Abigail, and that's why he was so upset—because someone knows his secret," Mandie said as she looked up at Joe.

"I don't know about that, but I'd love to get hold of whoever did write that message on the blackboard," Joe said, frowning. He added, "I just don't understand why Mr. Tallant wouldn't believe me."

"I'm sure your father will straighten him out when you tell him," Mandie said.

"I don't want my father having to straighten things out for me," Joe said. "I'm too old for that. I want Mr. Tallant to take my word as the truth."

"But he won't, so you'll have to tell your father," Mandie said.

"Oh, I'll tell my father, all right, but I will also ask

him about that extra key," Joe replied. "Someone has probably stolen it."

"Things get deeper and deeper, don't they?" Mandie said, and then added, "I'd like to know who is in my father's house, but I can't figure out how to find out."

"We'll just go up to the door and knock again. Maybe whoever is in there will decide to answer," Joe said.

"I sure hope so," Mandie said.

"We're getting close now, so I'd advise you to pick up Snowball and carry him, just in case the wild man sees us and starts acting crazy again," Joe told her.

Mandie quickly stooped and picked up her cat. "Snowball, you'd better behave," she told him. "We've got too many other things going on right now for you to run off again."

Joe looked down at the cat, who was looking intently up into his mistress's face.

When the house came into view, they circled by way of the barn, as they usually did, and stopped to look.

"There's still smoke coming out of the chimney," Mandie whispered to Joe as she held tightly to Snowball in her arms.

"And we haven't heard anything from the wild man yet," Joe said as he peered over her shoulder.

Mandie turned slightly and asked, "Well, do we walk up to the front door?"

"We can try it," Joe agreed. "I'll go first. You follow close behind me."

They darted from tree to tree for cover and finally made their way up to the front porch of the house. Finally having to come completely out of cover, Mandie felt tingles down her spine as she thought of the wild man. She and Joe were in full view.

"Let's try the front door first," Joe suggested, and walked toward the front steps.

Mandie followed as he went up the steps and walked toward the front door. He motioned for her to knock. She stepped closer and raised her fist to pound on the door. She paused with her fist in mid-air as she heard a shot strike the tin roof.

Joe immediately put his arm around her and reached for the door. He hit it as hard as he could and tried rattling the doorknob, but there was no response from inside.

"Let's go see if the shutter is still open on that window we looked through last night," Mandie whispered to him as she squeezed Snowball tight to keep him from escaping.

"Let me go first," Joe whispered back.

They hurried down the front steps and stooped low to walk around to the window. Mandie slowly stood up to look inside. The shutter was still open, but she couldn't see much because there was no light in the cabin.

"Knock on the glass," Joe whispered from behind her.

Mandie looked at him and then started pounding on the glass. She stopped and listened, but there was no sound from within. Joe reached around her and tried to force the window open, but it wouldn't budge.

The two crouched back down below the window.

"The only way to get in," said Mandie, "is to break a pane and go through the window—"

"Which we are not going to do," Joe interrupted her. "It's too dangerous and it's against the law."

Mandie looked at him and said, "I want to try the front door again."

She walked in a stooped position, trying to protect herself from any stray bullets, back to the front porch and then stood up at the front door. Joe followed.

Raising her hand this time, she pounded on the door and called out, "Open the door! Open up! I want to talk to you!"

Joe finally grabbed her hand, which was bruised from the pounding, and said, "It's no use. Either there is no one in there or they are not going to come to the door."

Mandie looked up at him and nodded. She was so full of disappointment she couldn't speak. She silently followed Joe across the yard and onto the main road. Snowball was trying to scratch, so Mandie finally let him down to walk at the end of his red leash.

"You still have some time left before you have to go back to school," Joe reminded her. "We'll keep coming back until we accomplish something one way or another."

"I've decided it must be an outlaw hiding in my father's house," Mandie said in a firm voice.

"Why do you think that?" Joe asked.

"Because they are so secretive. They won't answer the door and won't even say a word," she explained.

"Anyone who didn't want you to know they were in there would do that, Mandie, not just an outlaw," Joe replied.

"And that man who is shooting—he's probably friends with whoever is in there, and they probably had an argument, and now the one inside won't let the other in," Mandie went on.

Joe looked down at her and frowned. "You do have an imagination!" he said.

"It's just plain common sense if you'd stop and think about it," Mandie said. "Otherwise why would that man keep shooting at the house? And why won't whoever is inside open the door?"

"In that case we should contact the sheriff, as my mother suggested last night," Joe said. "Let's talk to my father about this."

"I hope he's still home," Mandie replied, as they walked down the road.

―――――

Joe left his rifle on the back porch. He and Mandie found Dr. Woodard sitting in a corner of the kitchen, reading a newspaper. His father looked up as the two came in through the back door.

"I knew y'all would be back as soon as you smelled food," he said, laughing.

"Long walks make me hungry," Joe said, also laughing.

"Me too," Mandie added as she set Snowball down and removed his red leash. He ran for the bowl next to the stove. "I believe Snowball is also hungry."

Mrs. Miller was helping Mrs. Woodard at the cookstove. She turned to ask, "Well, did y'all ever find that stranger you were looking for?"

Dr. and Mrs. Woodard immediately looked at the young people.

"What's this about looking for a stranger?" Mrs. Woodard asked.

"What stranger?" Dr. Woodard wanted to know.

Joe sat down on a stool by his father's chair. "It's a long story. You already know about the man who was shooting on the mountain. Well, when we went back, he was shooting again, and he was howling like an animal, then laughing like he had gone crazy."

All three adults focused their attention on Joe. Mandie dropped onto another footstool nearby.

"What are you talking about, Joe?" his mother asked as she stepped closer.

"We never did see the man, but he seemed to follow us around all over the mountain with this howling, shooting, and laughing," Joe said.

"And you don't have any idea as to who he is?" Dr. Woodard asked.

"No, sir," Joe said. He turned to Mandie and said, "Tell them what you know about it, Mandie."

Mandie looked at each adult and then said, "I think I heard him here around the house somewhere in the middle of last night." She stopped and waited for their reactions.

All three adults looked at each other and then at the young people.

"You heard him around the house here?" Mrs. Woodard asked.

"Are you sure about it?" Dr. Woodard said.

Mrs. Miller spoke up before Mandie could answer and said, "So that's what y'all were asking me about this morning. A strange man!"

"Well, I'm not positive I heard him," Mandie said. "I was so scared when all this happened yesterday and I had it on my mind when I went to bed. I might have dreamed it—but I don't think so." She watched and waited.

"We looked all over the yard and outbuildings and everywhere this morning, but we didn't find anything wrong or see anyone strange," Joe said.

"And you think this is the same person who is shooting at Mandie's father's house?" Dr. Woodard asked Joe.

Joe nodded and Mandie said, "Yes, sir."

"And you say there is someone in the house, and they won't come to the door?" Dr. Woodard continued.

"We think so, because someone is keeping a fire going in the fireplace," Joe replied.

"We can see the smoke coming out of the chimney, and the shutter on one window is open, so we can see the reflection of the fire in the fireplace, but we haven't been able to see anyone inside," Mandie added.

"Maybe we should call in the sheriff," Mrs. Woodard said.

"I don't know about that yet," Dr. Woodard said. "You can't arrest someone just for shooting a gun in the mountains, or laughing and carrying on like a wild man. But if the man comes here, then that is a different story."

Mrs. Woodard spoke up. "I don't like y'all going over there by yourselves," she said.

Joe said, "But, Mama, the man is not shooting at us. He's shooting at Mandie's father's house. And I've been taking my rifle with me."

"I can't go with y'all because I've got to go back across the mountain after we eat," Dr. Woodard said. "I'm afraid Gretchen does have the measles, and I'm worried that it might break out everywhere around here. I'm trying to keep close watch on anyone who comes down sick."

"I'm sorry about Gretchen," Joe said. Then he added, "But if you're going back over there right away, would you have a few minutes to talk to me about something before you go?"

Dr. Woodard looked at him in surprise and said, "Of course, son."

Mrs. Miller spoke up, "The food is ready now if y'all would like to eat."

Mrs. Woodard went back to the stove as she said, "Let's eat first, Joe. Then you can talk with your father."

"Yes, ma'am," Joe agreed.

Everyone hurried through the meal. Mandie could tell Mrs. Miller was anxious to get back to her house. And Joe was hurrying to talk with his father. And Dr. Woodard was rushing to get back across the mountain. And she wanted to know what the doctor would have to say about their encounter at the schoolhouse. Even Mrs. Woodard seemed to be hurrying for some reason, probably to give Joe time to talk after the meal.

When they were finished Dr. Woodard laid down his napkin and said, "All right, son, let's go outside." He rose from his chair as everyone else stood up.

Joe looked at Mandie and said, "Let me talk to my father first and then I think he will want to discuss everything with you."

"Go ahead. I'll wait in here," Mandie said.

Dr. Woodard and Joe went out the back door and Mandie turned to the two women to ask, "Is there anything I can do to help?"

"Oh no, dear," Mrs. Woodard said. "In fact we don't have much left to do. Mrs. Miller cleaned up at the stove and sink while we ate, and now I'm fixing food for her to take home."

"I'd be glad to help," Mandie said.

"I know what you can do, then," Mrs. Woodard said with a big smile. "Why don't you round up some scraps here and give them to your cat for its dinner?"

Mandie did as she suggested and ended up with a good-sized dinner for Snowball. She set it down by the stove, and he began growling and purring as he ate it.

In a few minutes Joe opened the door and called to Mandie, "Come on outside, Mandie."

She smiled at Mrs. Woodard and then went out the door.

Dr. Woodard was seated on a bench in the yard, and Mandie followed Joe to him.

"Sit down, Miss Amanda," the doctor said, patting the bench. "Plenty of room for all three of us."

"Thank you, Dr. Woodard," Mandie said as she sat on the end by Joe.

"Now Joe has been telling me about what went on at the schoolhouse this morning, and I want you to tell me your version of it," the doctor said.

"Yes, sir," Mandie said, and she related the facts about the incident with Mr. Tallant. "I just couldn't believe Mr. Tallant would doubt Joe's word," she ended.

"Now about that extra key," the doctor said, looking at the two. "I haven't told Joe this yet. I used that key over a year ago when we had a little festival in and around the schoolhouse while Mr. Tallant was gone on vacation. And I hate to say that I forgot and left it in the door. One of the Montgomery children fell out of a swing and got hurt, so nobody remembered to get the key. I have never thought to mention this to Mr. Tallant, but evidently someone just took the key. I haven't seen it since."

"What a relief!" Joe said with a big smile.

"Yes," Mandie agreed. "So anyone could have it."

"We need to have a conference with Mr. Tallant, but I have to go back over the mountain and am not sure when I'll get back," Dr. Woodard said. "And I don't want y'all doing anything to irritate Mr. Tallant while I'm gone."

"Yes, sir, I wouldn't be about to irritate Mr. Tallant. I want to stay away from him," Joe said.

"Me too," Mandie agreed.

"I think he will give you an apology," Dr. Woodard told Joe.

"Knowing about the extra key sure makes me feel better," Joe said.

Dr. Woodard looked at the two young people and said, "Now I'm not going to forbid y'all to go back over to the house where Miss Amanda lived with her father, but I am going to warn you both to be very careful. I know Miss Amanda will have to go back to school at the end of the week, and I don't want to curtail her activities while she's here, but please be alert."

"Yes, sir, thank you," Mandie told him.

"We will," Joe promised. "If we could just figure out who is inside the house before Mandie leaves!"

The three stood up.

"And you be sure you carry your rifle at all times, Joe," Dr. Woodard added. "Now I've got to get back inside and get ready to leave."

"Thanks, Dad," Joe said as he reached to quickly put an arm around his father's shoulders. "And you be careful, too."

"I always try to be," the doctor said.

As the three went back inside, they met Mrs. Miller coming out. Her arms were filled with covered dishes of food.

"Y'all be careful now," Mrs. Miller said as she passed them.

"You too," Mandie and Joe called back to her.

Dr. Woodard got his medical bag and left immediately. Mandie and Joe sat down with Joe's mother long enough to explain what the conference with his father had been about.

"There are some strange things going on around here lately," Mrs. Woodard said.

"That's exactly what I've been saying," Mandie agreed.

Joe stood up and said, "And I suppose now we're ready to go back to your father's house."

"Right," Mandie said as she, too, rose. She looked at Snowball.

Mrs. Woodard noticed her glance and said, "Leave him here if you wish, dear. I'll look after him."

"Thanks, Mrs. Woodard," Mandie said with a big smile. She was glad to be relieved of one big problem.

Mrs. Woodard also rose. "Now don't y'all stay gone too long. I'll be worried about you," she told them.

"We won't," Joe promised.

"Without Snowball we can move faster," Mandie said.

The two young people went outside, where Joe picked up his rifle.

"We need to make plans before we get there this time," Joe said.

"I don't know how to make any plans. Nothing seems to go as we plan it," Mandie said.

"Let's sit down over here and discuss what we want to do," Joe said.

The two sat on a bench in the yard and talked about what they would do when they got to Mandie's father's house this time.

Chapter 10 / The Culprit

"We'll just go right up to the front door and beat and bang all afternoon until someone comes to the door. If we make enough racket, whoever is inside is bound to get tired of it and open the door to tell us to stop," Mandie suggested.

"We can try it, but that may not work. I just wish there were other houses, other people living close to your father's house. Then maybe someone would know who's in there," Joe remarked.

"With a hundred and twenty acres belonging to my father, and most of it along the road, there couldn't be any neighbors really close," Mandie replied. With a sad expression on her face she added, "He always told me that's why he bought it in the first place, so there wouldn't be other people so close. Just like y'all don't have any neighbors close."

"One reason for that is not many people come to live in this part of the mountains," Joe said. "Most of the land is not good enough to make a living on it."

"Well, anyhow, don't you think we'd better get started?" Mandie asked.

"I suppose so," Joe agreed as he picked up his rifle and rose.

Mandie stood up and said, "I'm ready."

The two walked out to the main road and on in the direction of Mandie's father's house. Mandie insisted that Joe stop now and then to call his dog. He seemed to have given up on finding her, but Mandie felt if they kept looking, eventually Samantha would show up.

"Joe, you've got to keep looking for Samantha," Mandie said as Joe stood in the middle of the road. "Remember, she's probably somewhere in trouble and needs your help. You said yourself she wouldn't just run off and leave her babies."

"I know," Joe said, kicking the dust on the dirt road. "I'm not giving up. It's just that I don't know what to do next to find her. I don't believe she is within the sound of my whistle or she would come to me."

"Unless she can't," Mandie said. "Remember Snowball was stuck in the cornfield with his leash hung up on those cornstalks? Well, Samantha could be stuck somewhere."

"But if she is, and if she could hear me, I think she would make some noise to let me know she heard," Joe said.

"And suppose she is hurt, or something, and is not able to bark or whine," Mandie reminded him.

"All right, I know I'll keep on looking, even if I never find her," Joe said. He whirled around and whistled so loudly the birds in the bushes nearby suddenly took flight.

The two waited for a few minutes and then silently walked on down the road. They stopped now and then and Joe called Samantha, but there was no response.

When they came within sight of Mandie's father's house they circled by the barn as they usually did. Hiding behind the corner of the building, they watched the house for a while.

"There's still smoke coming out of the chimney," Mandie whispered. "And no sign of anyone around. And I haven't heard any shots."

"But the minute we start knocking on that front door I imagine that wild man will start shooting," Joe replied. "For some reason that man, whoever he is, doesn't want us near the house."

"But he can't stop us," Mandie said.

"Unless he shoots us," Joe said.

Mandie whirled around to look at Joe in alarm. "You don't think he would really shoot us, do you?" she asked.

"I have no idea, but as wild as he seems to be I wouldn't put anything past him," Joe told her. "Therefore, we've got to be careful and alert every minute, remember that."

Mandie felt her heartbeat quicken. She had not really thought much about the situation since the man seemed intent on shooting at the roof of the house. He'd had lots of chances to aim at them but had not.

"Joe, our verse," she said, reaching back for Joe's hand.

Together they repeated, "What time I am afraid I will put my trust in Thee." Mandie straightened her shoulder, looked up at Joe and said, "Come on. I'm ready now to knock on the front door."

They darted from tree to tree and made their way to the front porch. Mandie rushed across to the front door and began pounding on it with both fists. Joe reached over her head and helped. They kept on and on for a few minutes without any response. Finally Mandie stopped to look at her fists.

"Wow!" she said. "I think I've bruised my hands. Look how red they are."

Joe looked at hers and then his. "I probably did, too, but it'll go away," he said. "Mandie, we are just not going to be able to get someone to the door. You might as well give up on it."

At that moment a shot rang out on the tin roof above. Joe quickly put his arm around Mandie and said, "Let's get off this porch."

He led the way as they walked in a stooped position down the steps and around to the side away from the direction the shots seemed to be coming from. They sat down on the ground. Joe held on to his rifle.

"Let's go back to the barn where we'll have some protection and watch and see if the man keeps shooting," Mandie suggested.

"All right, but we'd better make a quick path across the yard," Joe told her.

After they got safely to the barn they watched the house and listened for more shots, but nothing happened.

"You see what I mean?" Joe told her. "Whoever that is shooting just doesn't want us near the house."

"And I wonder why," Mandie said as she kept listening.

Suddenly the air seemed to fill with smoke and Mandie cried out as she looked at the chimney of the house. "Joe! There's something wrong! Look at all the smoke coming out of the chimney!"

"Someone must have an awfully big fire in the

fireplace," Joe remarked as he watched.

In only minutes the whole house seemed to be engulfed in smoke. Mandie and Joe coughed as it drifted toward them.

"Let's go, Joe! We've got to do something! The house must be on fire!" Mandie cried out as she suddenly raced toward the house. Joe left his rifle leaning against the barn and rushed after her. Circling the house until they came to the window with the shutter open, they tried to look inside but the smoke was too thick.

"Let's break the glass! Someone must be in there!" Mandie exclaimed as she looked around for something to knock out the window.

Joe picked up a large rock and pushed Mandie aside. "Watch out for glass splinters!" he yelled at her as he threw the rock with all his strength into the glass window.

Glass flew through the air and Joe pushed Mandie to the ground to shield her. As it settled they looked up. There was a large hole where the glass panes had been, but the edge held jagged glass.

"Wait!" Joe quickly told Mandie as she started toward the window. "I've got to clean out the loose glass." He snatched a rough limb lying nearby and began banging away at the broken edges.

Smoke was pouring out the broken window now. Mandie put her handkerchief over her nose and said, "Let's go inside!"

The window was low to the ground, but Joe pushed an old milk can under the opening.

"I'd better go first," Joe said.

Mandie hesitated and then she said, "Be sure you reach back for me when you get inside." Her heart was running away, not only from the smoke and the possibility of someone inside the house but from the realization that she was about to enter her father's house for the first time since she had been farmed out to another family when her father died.

Joe jumped through and turned back to assist Mandie. She didn't even look for shattered glass but tumbled through and landed on her feet. The smoke was so thick she couldn't see anything inside. She and Joe began feeling their way around.

"Keep your nose covered," Joe warned from behind his handkerchief.

Mandie did as he said and used her other hand to find the way into the living room where the fireplace was. As she looked in the doorway she screamed in fear. Flames were eating at the boards of the floor in front of the fireplace. She grabbed at a quilt lying nearby to beat the fire, then suddenly realized some-one was under the quilt. She jumped back.

"Joe! Someone's there!" she cried behind the handkerchief over her nose as she jerked at Joe's hand.

Joe quickly bent and threw the quilt back. Man-die watched and gasped.

"It's Irene!" she cried. She stooped down and tried to speak to the girl. "Irene, Irene, it's Mandie! Wake up!" She gave the girl a little push, but Irene didn't move.

"I think she's overcome with smoke," Joe said. "We've got to get out of here."

Suddenly Mandie was aware of another pres-ence in the smoke-filled room. She tried to see who it was. Then the person roughly pushed her aside and knelt by Irene.

"Irene, my love," the voice said, and Mandie in-stantly recognized Nimrod.

"Nimrod, it's me, Mandie," she said. "We've got to get her out of here."

Nimrod yelled at her. "I can see that," he said.

"I'll help you get her out the window," Joe said as he stooped beside Nimrod.

Nimrod had picked Irene up, quilt and all, and was walking toward the broken window. Joe quickly followed and jumped outside ahead of him. Mandie stayed behind as she tried to beat out the flames on the floorboards.

"Hand her to me and then you can jump out," Joe told Nimrod.

"Be sure you don't drop her," Nimrod ordered in a rough voice as he pushed Irene through the window and Joe caught her on the outside.

Nimrod jumped out behind her and Joe quickly climbed back inside.

"Joe, we've got to put this fire out. The whole house will burn down," Mandie cried as she frantically beat the flames with anything she could get her hands on.

Joe began jerking down curtains and using them to beat out the flames. And they were both surprised to see Nimrod come back in and help.

"It's out. Now I have to get Irene home," Nimrod told them as the last tiny flame disappeared. He coughed from the smoke.

Mandie fought for her breath and no one had to tell her to get out the window into fresh air. Joe followed her. Then Nimrod jumped outside. He was coughing and breathing hard as he rushed toward Irene where he had laid her on the quilt under a tree. He stooped to pick her up.

"Where are you taking her, Nimrod?" Joe asked.

The huge, tall man, now grown much larger

since Mandie had seen him, turned to look at them and said, "Home."

"Home?" Mandie questioned. "Doesn't Irene live here anymore?"

"Not since we got married this summer," Nimrod explained. "She moved in the house with me and then she had to go and get mad about something, and I don't even know what it was, and she ran away and came back here. But now I'm taking her home."

"Where are her mother and Zack Hughes?" Mandie asked as she blew black out of her nose.

"Them? Oh, they left a long time ago. Went to live in his old house over in the next county," Nimrod said. "Now I'll be going."

Joe stepped up to his side and asked, "Would you like for me to go get a wagon, or a horse? It would be easier to move her."

"Nope, ain't got time for that," Nimrod said as he looked down at the limp form in his arms. "Got to get her brung to." He started to walk on.

"So you are the one who has been shooting at the house?" Mandie questioned.

Nimrod paused and looked back. "Sure, it was me. I tried to scare her out, but it didn't work, only scared you and Joe here." He laughed his wild laugh.

Mandie and Joe quickly looked at each other. Mandie could read Joe's mind. He wanted to even scores with Nimrod, but under the circumstances it was better not to start something.

"I think we'd better follow him," Joe said, stepping up beside Mandie. "Even though I don't want to, I'm afraid he may need some help getting Irene to his house."

"You're right," Mandie agreed. "It wouldn't do any good to start a fuss now over the way Nimrod has been shooting and acting wild."

She looked back at her father's house, which was still enveloped in smoke. Joe noticed this and said, "We'll come back later when the smoke has cleared out."

Nimrod turned to look at the two who were following him down the road. He slowed his steps as though he were coming back to them, but then he turned away and silently carried Irene in his arms.

They had not gone far when a cart showed up in the distance, heading toward them.

"Maybe we can get some help," Joe remarked as he squinted to see who it was.

"Why, it's Miss Abigail!" Mandie said, quickly waving to the woman.

Miss Abigail slowed down and stopped by the two and then looked at Nimrod walking on. "What's going on? Y'all looks as though you've been down the chimney. And what is Nimrod doing?"

"Oh, Miss Abigail, could you please give Nimrod a ride to his house? He's carrying Irene. My father's house was on fire and we broke in and found Irene. She's just plain passed out," Mandie hurriedly tried to explain.

"And Nimrod happened to come to the house after we did. He says he and Irene are married," Joe said.

"Yes, that's right. Here, let me help," she said as she quickly turned her cart around and stopped beside Nimrod. The man turned, saw who it was, and paused. Mandie and Joe raced after her.

"Nimrod, put Irene in here and we can carry her home," Miss Abigail said.

Nimrod didn't hesitate but carefully laid Irene in the back of the cart as everyone watched. Then he reached into his pocket and pulled out a large key.

"Here, Miss Abigail, here's your key," Nimrod said, handing her the key. "I wrote on the blackboard like you told me to."

Mandie and Joe instantly gasped and looked at each other. So Nimrod was the culprit.

Miss Abigail took the key and dropped it into her little bag. "Thank you, Nimrod," she said. And then with a big smile she added, "It worked. Mr. Tallant has asked me to marry him. The wedding will be next spring."

Mandie and Joe looked at each other in disbelief. This supposedly shy woman had done such a thing to get herself a husband, Mandie was thinking. How could she?

"Miss Abigail, might I ask where you got the key to the schoolhouse?" Joe ventured.

The old maid lady fluttered her eyelids and said, "Why, Joe, your father left the key in the door a while back at the festival. Remember the festival? I found it and just haven't remembered to give it to Dr. Woodard, but I will soon."

Mandie wondered why she didn't give it to Joe to pass on to his father, but then the woman seemed to have some strange ideas.

"Miss Abigail, we need to get my Irene home," Nimrod reminded her as he swung over the edge and into the cart.

Miss Abigail looked at Mandie and Joe and said, "Perhaps you two could squeeze in back there."

"Oh no, thank you, Miss Abigail, we'll walk on," Mandie said. "It won't take us long. Thank you anyhow."

Miss Abigail waved and drove her cart on ahead.

"Well, looks like we've solved more than one

mystery," Mandie remarked as she looked up at Joe. "I'd like to see Mr. Tallant's face when he finds out his lady love finagled a proposal out of him—and not only that, she had the key that he was blaming us for stealing."

Joe stopped to catch Mandie's hand. "Look, Mandie," he said. "There's no use in our knowledge about the proposal going any further. It will be enough just to let Mr. Tallant know that she had the key all the time. He can figure things out for himself."

"I suppose you're right. I'm just amazed Miss Abigail would do such a thing, and she didn't seem to mind that we overheard everything," Mandie replied.

Joe gave Mandie's face a sudden brush with his hand and then laughed. "You need a bath, young lady! As Miss Abigail said, you do look like you've been down the chimney."

Mandie jerked his hand and also began laughing. "Include yourself, Mr. Joe Woodard! Your mother is going to have fits when she sees you."

Mandie felt a burden lifted now that she had finally been able to get inside her father's house, but she was wondering about what would happen next.

She quit laughing and frowned as they walked on. "Joe, if Irene's mother and her husband, Zack Hughes, have moved to his house, and if Irene has married Nimrod and is living with him, my father's house is empty." She gasped with excitement.

"So what are you going to do about it?" Joe asked as he looked down at her with a serious expression.

"Do? Why, I don't know," Mandie replied. "You're going to be a lawyer. Who would the house belong to now?"

Joe cleared his throat and said, "That would depend on your father's will. Did he make a will leaving the property to your stepmother?"

Mandie thought about that quickly. "I don't know anything about any will at all. My father died and my stepmother just sent me to live with the Brysons, then she married Zack Hughes and he moved in the house with her."

"You could talk to Irene later when she's recovered from the smoke," Joe said. "Maybe she knows something about it."

"Well, exactly how were you planning to get his house back for me if I agreed to marry you when we grow up?" Mandie asked.

"I would have to go through law school to learn how to do that, but it could be done because you are your father's only daughter. Irene is your stepmother's daughter by a previous marriage and not even related to your father—unless he took out papers adopting her as his daughter," Joe tried to explain.

They were within sight of the Woodards' house and Mandie said, "Sounds too complicated. Let's hurry and get cleaned up and go back to my father's house."

As they hurried down the driveway they found Mrs. Woodard evidently returning from the barn with a pan in her hands. She stopped in astonishment as she saw the two.

"What on earth happened to y'all? Are you hurt?" she exclaimed as she gazed at their dirty faces and clothes.

"No, ma'am, we're not hurt," Joe said. "Let's go inside where I can get a drink of water and we'll explain what happened."

As they stood in the kitchen drinking water Mandie realized they were too dirty to sit in a chair. They hurriedly explained where they had been and what had transpired since they left home.

Mrs. Woodard gasped in shock. "You could have been burned to death or suffocated by all that fire and smoke," she said. "Now both of you, get cleaned up, fast."

"Yes, ma'am," the two chorused.

"As soon as we eat we want to go back and look inside my father's house," Mandie said as she and Joe started for the hallway door.

"No," Mrs. Woodard said so firmly the two stopped and looked at her. "This is one time I forbid you to go back. The house will still be full of smoke and hot ashes, or whatever, and you could be injured. So just clean up and get to the table."

"Oh, Mama!" Joe said with a moan. "Couldn't we go just for a few minutes?"

"No, I said no, and I mean it," Mrs. Woodard said, going to the cookstove. "Your father is not home and he sent word he probably wouldn't be back until Saturday and I'm not going to be responsible for the two of you going back to that house."

"Yes, ma'am," Mandie said with a disappointed sigh. "I understand."

"All right," Joe agreed.

Mandie was itching with impatience to get back to her father's house and look inside, but she knew she would have to wait until morning. Well, anyway, by then the smoke would have disappeared and she would be able to spend time inside the house.

Chapter 11 / The Secret of the Fire

While they ate supper that night, Mandie and Joe told Mrs. Woodard about their adventures during the day.

Mrs. Woodard couldn't keep from laughing. "Do you mean that shy Miss Abigail did all this? She must be leading two lives. I hope Mr. Tallant knows what he is getting when he marries her," she said. "The outcome will be interesting."

Mandie explained about the fire and their rescuing Irene.

"She was completely overcome by smoke," Joe said. "Anyway Nimrod will take good care of her, I imagine."

After they had discussed everything they could think of, Mandie asked, "Will you give us permission to go back to the house tomorrow, Mrs. Woodard?"

Mrs. Woodard cleared her throat and hesitated a moment before she said, "Well, I suppose so. I just don't want y'all getting into trouble or getting hurt or something while the doctor is away, and he probably won't be home until the day after tomorrow."

"I'll take good care of Mandie, Mama," Joe promised.

Mandie laughed and looked at Joe. "And I'll take good care of Joe."

"All right then, but I don't want y'all gone too long at a time," Mrs. Woodard replied. "Now tonight we have apple cobbler for dessert. How about it?"

Mandie and Joe both ran to the warmer to get it.

Mandie said, "I'm sure going to miss all this wonderful food when I go back to school." Joe carried the warm pan to the table and set it on hot mats.

"I think we should all go to bed early tonight because I know y'all want to get up early in the morning," Mrs. Woodard said. "So let's make hay with this pie."

They did go to bed early that night, but Mandie was so excited about getting into her father's house she couldn't go to sleep for a long time after she went to bed. She had all sorts of questions. Would there be anything left that had belonged to her father? Would it look the same as when she had lived there? The smoke had been so thick and there had been so much excitement that she had not even taken a glimpse around the rooms.

Finally morning came, and Mandie was up with the birds. She quickly dressed, picked up Snowball, and opened the door to go downstairs. At the same time Joe, who was also walking down the hallway, looked back and waited for her.

"Do you know if your mother will be up for breakfast? Or if we can just go on to my father's house as soon as we eat?" Mandie asked as they went down the steps.

"Don't you smell that bacon and coffee?" Joe teased. "That's Mrs. Miller's trademark. She's cooking breakfast, which means my mother will be sleeping late. Therefore we can leave anytime we get ready." He pushed open the kitchen door for Mandie to enter ahead of him. Mandie set Snowball down.

After exchanging greetings with Mrs. Miller, the two rushed to the table and sat down. "I see y'all are in a hurry, so I'll hurry," Mrs. Miller said as she began placing dishes of hot food on the table. "Joe, you grab that coffeepot down there and pour y'all's coffee." She put a bowl of food on the floor for Snowball, who began eating hungrily.

Mandie fastened on Snowball's leash and picked him up after they had eaten. They told Mrs. Miller goodbye and went out the back door. Joe picked up his rifle from the shed in the yard, where he had put it the night before.

"Do you think you need to take that rifle now that we know who the wild man is and that he won't hurt us?" Mandie asked.

"Yes, because my father told me to be sure I took it with me, remember?" Joe said as they walked down the driveway.

Mandie didn't talk much on the way. She walked fast, and Snowball tried his best to get down, but she held him firmly in her arms. And when the house came into view, Mandie broke into a run. Joe rushed after her as she went around to the window they had broken.

"Wait, Mandie!" he called to her. "I'll go through that window and open the front door so you won't get your clothes all dirty." He leaned his rifle against a tree and ran over to the window.

Mandie looked at the soot-covered windowsill and said, "All right, but if you aren't careful you'll get all blacked up."

"I have longer legs and can step in easier," Joe said as he stepped up on an old milk can beneath the window.

Mandie watched until he went over the sill. Then she raced around to the front door. Joe had it open by the time she got there.

She got as far as the doorway and stopped abruptly. Snowball took the opportunity to jump down from her arms and wander into the house. Tears filled Mandie's blue eyes, and she tried to calm her emotions. Joe reached for her hand.

"Come on in, Mandie," Joe told her. "It takes only about two steps to do it."

Mandie glanced up at him through misty eyes and allowed him to gently pull her through the doorway. She stopped again and looked around. Everything seemed the way it had been when she was sent away from home. There were the two rocking chairs where her father and Etta had sat before the fireplace. Even the blue cushions were still on them, though they looked worn and dirty. And there was the low stool where she had sat at her father's knee while he read to her.

"It's still the same, isn't it?" Joe asked. He, too, had been in the Shaw house numerous times when Mandie lived there.

Mandie nodded, unable to speak. She wandered through the rest of the house and came back to the living room. She had been in such a daze she had not even noticed the damage the fire had done.

"I think we were lucky," Joe said, bending over to look at the floor in front of the fireplace. "These burned boards here can be easily replaced."

Mandie stooped to inspect the damage. "Yes, I think they could," she said, and then she remembered something her father had said long ago—"Mandie, this is a secret trap door where I keep all my important papers and things," he had said, pointing to the boards in front of the fireplace. "Always remember that, and don't ever let anyone else know about it."

Etta and Irene had been gone somewhere and she had been home alone with her father. He had shown her how to open it and then close it back up.

Now Mandie became excited as she told Joe about it. "There's a secret trap door along about here where my father kept important things. Come on. Let's find it."

She went down on her knees and began poking at the row of boards that were burned. The flames had spread out probably three feet from the stone hearth.

"How are we supposed to get it open?" Joe asked, puzzled as he looked at the floor.

"We need something long, thin, and sharp," Mandie finally said as she looked around the room.

Joe jumped up and said, "A butcher knife, if there is one in the kitchen. I'll look." He went out of the room.

By the time he came back, Mandie had decided which boards were made to open. She showed him, and he pried between the boards with the long knife. After a struggle the two were able to lift the secret door.

A metal box was sitting on a shelflike space beneath the floor. Mandie eagerly reached for it. She found it was heavy, so Joe helped her pull it out. Setting it on the floor, she tried to open it, but the lid seemed stuck.

"Oh shucks!" she exclaimed.

"Let me see if I can get it open," Joe offered as he reached for the box. He tried too, but it did seem to be stuck. "I know," he added, reaching for the knife he had laid aside. "I'll try the knife." He ran the butcher knife under the edge of the lid and, after a while, was able to get the lid up. He didn't open the box all the way but handed it back to Mandie.

Mandie took it and quickly threw the lid open. It seemed to be full of legal-looking papers. She took out the top one and read out loud, "Deed." She looked up at Joe and said, "These must be the papers where he bought this property." She handed it to him.

"It sure is," Joe confirmed as he unfolded and read the pages. "This says he bought the place in 1888, the year you were born, from a Mr. Tindall."

Mandie reached back into the box and found an envelope of old photographs, which she quickly shuffled through. "I don't know who all these people are, but I'm sure Uncle John will know."

She took out more papers. "And here is a marriage license for him and Etta, and here is a Bible." She took it out and fanned through the pages. "I think all the family records are in here."

She passed everything to Joe to read. Finally she came to the last paper in the box. "This says 'Last Will and Testament of James Alexander Shaw.' Joe, you're going to be a lawyer. You'll have to go through all these for me later and tell me everything that it says." She handed the will to Joe.

Joe opened the document and silently read through it. Looking up at Mandie, he said, "You need to read this for yourself. Just skip the legal language in the first paragraph and read the second one." He handed her the paper and watched as she read it.

She read aloud, " 'I will and bequeath to my only heir, my daughter Amanda Elizabeth Shaw, the property I have just bought from Mr. Tindall, all of my personal effects, and any other property, both personal and real, that I may own or inherit here-after. . . . ' Joe, do you understand this the way I do?" She paused for it to all sink in.

"Yes, I understand it perfectly. You own this house and land," Joe said, anxiously watching her.

Mandie's face broke into a big smile as she said, "I do?" Then she looked at Joe and said, "Then I don't have to marry you when we grow up to get this house back."

Joe didn't say a word, and she looked sharply at him. "Isn't that what this means? That I don't have to get this house back, because I own it already?" she asked.

Joe shrugged his shoulders and stood up. "Yep, that's right." He sat down on a stool near the front door.

Mandie was so absorbed in what she had found that she didn't notice Joe's strange behavior. She carefully refolded the papers and put everything back into the metal box.

Snowball came nosing around the box, and Mandie suddenly realized he had been running loose with the door open and a hole in the window. She grabbed the end of his leash and stood up.

Mandie looked at Joe, who had become uncommonly quiet. "Don't you think we ought to go by Nimrod's and see how Irene is? Then I can tell her what I've found, that I own this house now," she said.

"Sure, why not?" Joe replied as he rose. "Did you notice there's a key inside in the front door? We can fasten the shutter over the broken window and then go out the front door and lock it."

"Yes, that's good," Mandie agreed. She left the box on the floor, held on to Snowball's leash, and followed Joe into the kitchen, where the broken window was.

"Now I see why this shutter was not closed," Joe said, examining the window. "It's broken. I need something to hammer with." He looked around the room and found a heavy piece of wood beside the cookstove.

"Here, I'll hold up the shutter while you hammer," Mandie said as they placed the shutter over the window.

"You see the nails are still in it, and all I'll have to do is pound them into the window facing," Joe explained as he began hitting a nail in the shutter with the piece of wood.

Mandie watched as the nail slowly went into the facing. Then Joe closed the latch on the inside and stood up. "All done," he said.

As they went back into the living room, Joe reached down and picked up the metal box. "I'll carry this for you. It's a little heavy," he said.

He took the key out of the inside keyhole in the front door and inserted it into the outside, pulled the door shut, and locked it. Handing Mandie the key, he said, "It's all yours now."

Mandie took the big key and looked it over. She

didn't remember the door ever being locked when she lived here. "Thanks," she said, looking up at Joe, who was already going down the front steps.

When she reached the yard, Mandie turned to take a final look at the house. Her father's house was all hers now. She owned it. And she wouldn't have to wait until she and Joe grew up to get it back.

"You coming?" Joe called from across the yard. He picked up his rifle from beside the tree where he had left it.

"I'm coming," Mandie called back, and ran to catch up with him. Snowball squirmed in her arms. "You're not getting down to run off again," she told the cat.

———

Mandie had never been to Nimrod's house before, but she knew where it was. As they got closer, she was surprised to see it was a neat little log cabin, probably two rooms at the most. The yard was clean, and she could see a storm cellar in the backyard with flowers blooming nearby. She couldn't imagine Nimrod taking care of a yard so nicely, so she figured Irene had probably done all the work.

Joe leaned his rifle against a tree and then tapped on the front door, which was closed. Mandie waited behind him with Snowball in her arms. Nimrod took his time answering the knock. Finally he opened the door just enough to see who was on the porch.

"Well?" he asked, not offering to open the door all the way.

Mandie stepped in front of Joe and said, "We just wanted to see how Irene is," she said.

"She's still sick and she's still asleep," Nimrod replied.

"Will you tell her we came by and that we found a box in the house," Mandie said, pointing to the metal box Joe was carrying. "There are legal papers in there saying I own my father's house, so we closed it up and locked it."

Nimrod frowned angrily. "What do you mean you *own* that house? Irene and her mother own that house," he said.

"No," Joe said. "We found Mandie's father's will in that box giving everything to Mandie."

"Well, I wouldn't be so sure about that," Nimrod said angrily as he slammed the door shut.

The sudden movement caused Snowball to jump down from Mandie's arms, and he quickly ran off to the backyard. Mandie and Joe followed, and by the time they found him, he was sitting by the storm cellar door hissing angrily, his fur raised on his back.

"What is he doing?" Mandie said as she went toward him. "Snowball, you come here, you hear?"

Joe followed and watched as Mandie tried to pick up the cat.

"Oh, you've gone and tangled up your leash again," Mandie said as she bent to untangle it.

Joe set the metal box down and stooped beside her. "Here, I'll help you," he said, pulling on the red leash.

Mandie tried to hold on to Snowball, but to her great surprise, he turned on her and fought with his front claws.

"Snowball, what has come over you?" she demanded as she slapped at his paws. "Don't you dare stick those claws into me."

But Snowball continued hissing and was now growling. His fur still stood up on his back. Mandie backed off a little and looked at him, then stomped her feet on the wooden frame of the storm cellar door which was made flat on the ground. She stopped suddenly and said, "Did you hear something?" She looked at Joe, who was still working on the leash.

"I thought I did, but I'm not sure," he said.

Snowball tried to scratch Joe, and Mandie stomped her feet again on the board frame. This time she halted and quickly looked at Joe. He had stopped with the leash and said, "There's something in the storm cellar, probably a wild animal." He tried to see down through a hole in the rotten wood.

The noise came again and this time Mandie said, "Whatever it is, Snowball doesn't like it. Let's open the door."

Mandie quickly unbuckled Snowball's collar so she could pick him up, because the leash was still tangled on the door hinge. Joe reached for the door handle.

"Stand back now," he said. "It could be a wild animal in there."

Mandie stepped back a little and watched. Joe managed to open the door, even though it was sagging on its hinges. And as he looked down into the cellar Mandie saw his face light up. He practically screamed, "Samantha!" He fell on his knees to reach down into the cellar. The steps had rotted and fallen away.

"Samantha! In there!" Mandie cried for joy. Joe had found his dog. She moved closer to look inside.

Joe was lying down trying to reach Samantha,

and the dog was weakly whining.

"Is she all right? Is she all right?" Mandie asked excitedly.

"Can't tell yet," Joe said as he slid halfway into the cellar. Calling back to Mandie, he said, "Hold on to my feet so I don't fall in."

Mandie quickly set Snowball down and grabbed Joe's feet. Joe moved around and she was afraid he would fall the rest of the way in, but he finally called back to Mandie. "I've got her. Help me wiggle backward out of here."

Mandie pulled on his feet as he pushed backward and at last his head came into sight. He managed to set Samantha on the ground when he got the rest of the way out. He quickly rolled over and hugged his dog.

"Samantha, girl, I love you," he cried, with tears in his voice.

Mandie noticed that Samantha was not moving very much and she asked, "Joe look at her. Is she all right?"

Joe immediately rolled over and rose to a stooping position. Samantha had livened up then enough to whine and try to lick his face.

In the meantime, Mandie had forgotten about Snowball, but she quickly looked around and found him sitting behind her, watching the dog. He was not even hissing. Evidently he could sense the dog's problem. Mandie snatched him up and managed to pull his leash away from the storm door. She quickly buckled on his collar. He didn't protest, but kept watching Samantha.

"I believe she's just starved," Joe said. "She probably hasn't had anything to eat since we missed her." He kept rubbing the dog's head, and

Samantha kept trying to lick his face.

"How do you think she got down in there?" Mandie asked.

Joe immediately became angry and said, "This storm cellar belongs to Nimrod, and I'm going back in that house to have it out with him. He either put Samantha in there or he must have known she was trapped in there." He stood up and clenched his fists.

Mandie grabbed his arm. "Wait, Joe! Don't go back to the house! Nimrod is a lot bigger than you are, and what if he hurt you so you wouldn't be able to get Samantha home? Think about her. She needs to go home as fast as you can carry her. From the looks of her, she would not be able to walk that far."

Joe removed her hand from his arm and said, "You're right. Let's get going. I need to take care of Samantha." He looked down at his dog and started to walk away as he called, "Come on, Samantha. Come on, girl. Let's go home."

Samantha managed to get to her feet, but she wobbled when she tried to come to him. Joe immediately took her into his arms. "That's all right, girl. I'll carry you home." He picked up the metal box in one hand.

They started back to the front yard. Mandie noticed Joe's rifle still standing by the tree. "Don't forget your rifle," she said. "Let me carry that box. You can't manage everything." She reached for it.

"I suppose it would be easier for you to carry the box than my rifle," Joe said as he handed the box to her and walked over to pick up his rifle.

The two were loaded down, but they soon made it back to the Woodards' house. Joe took Samantha into the kitchen and set her down near the cook-stove.

"Oh, Joe, I'm so glad you found her," his mother said, stooping to pet Samantha. The dog tried to lick her face also. "I believe she is starving and is just dying for some water."

Mrs. Woodard rushed across the room and filled a bowl with water, which she placed before the dog. Samantha thirstily drank and wagged her tail.

"Now let me see what I can find for her to eat," Mrs. Woodard said. She got a piece of ham from the warmer on the stove and placed it on a plate for the dog. Samantha quickly chewed and swallowed it.

Joe stood back and watched. "Thank goodness she's all right. If she can drink and eat like that she'll be all right."

In the meantime, Mandie had removed Snowball's leash and put him down. He just sat and watched the dog.

By the time the two young people told their stories to Mrs. Woodard, it was time for supper.

And when Mandie went to bed that night she thanked the Lord for her father's house. Even though he was gone, her father had provided for her. No matter what she would inherit back in Franklin from her mother or Uncle John, this inheritance was the most important thing in her life.

Chapter 12 / Sad News

The next morning Mandie woke early. She rushed to check the metal box to be sure it was still in the corner by the bureau. She thought she had put it there the night before, but she was afraid that her memories were just part of a fantastic dream. She opened the box and looked at the will on top of the papers. Her father's house was really hers.

She dressed quickly, took Snowball, and went down to the kitchen. Joe was nowhere around—probably still asleep, she thought. But Mrs. Miller was there, and from the smell in the air, Mandie could tell she was preparing another delicious breakfast.

"Good morning," she greeted Mrs. Miller, who was over by the stove. She set Snowball down and he immediately went to his plate, which still had scraps on it.

"Good morning," the woman said, stirring the

contents of a pot, which Mandie decided must be grits.

"Is anyone else up yet?" Mandie asked as she came over to stand by the stove and watch.

"Haven't seen a soul until you walked through that door," Mrs. Miller replied, bending to remove hot biscuits from the oven. She straightened up and added, "But then that's natural around here. With the doctor being a doctor, nothing is ever on a schedule."

"That's fine with me. I don't like schedules," Mandie said with a little laugh.

"Now if you'll just go sit down at the table I'll bring the food to you," Mrs. Miller said.

"I have a better idea," Mandie quickly said. "Why don't I just bring my plate over here to the stove and you can put some food on it. That way everything will stay warm for everybody else."

"Well, that's a right bright idea, if you don't mind doing that," Mrs. Miller agreed.

Mandie hurried to the table, got a plate, and walked back over to the stove. She held it out and said, "I eat anything, so put whatever you want on it. I'm not picky."

"That's nice to know," Mrs. Miller said, opening pot lids and uncovering frying pans as she heaped bacon, eggs, grits, and hot biscuits onto the plate.

"Wow!" Mandie exclaimed as she looked at the hearty portions of food. "I should have said a *little bit* of everything."

She carried her plate to the table and sat down. Mrs. Miller hurried over with the coffeepot and filled her cup.

"Now there's marmalade and honey sitting on

the table there," Mrs. Miller told her. "And there's the butter."

"Yes, ma'am, thank you," Mandie said as she began buttering her biscuit.

Suddenly she remembered Samantha. Joe had left her in the kitchen for the night. But where was she now?

"Mrs. Miller, have you seen Samantha this morning?" she asked as she bit into her biscuit.

"Why no, have y'all found her?" the woman asked.

"Oh, you don't even know! Yes, we found her yesterday afternoon," Mandie explained as she told Mrs. Miller about where they had found her.

"You don't say!" Mrs. Miller remarked, sitting down by the cookstove.

At that moment Joe came in the back door with a smile on his face. "I took Samantha out to her puppies a while ago, and was she happy to see them!"

"I'm so glad she's better now," Mandie said. "Have you eaten yet? Mrs. Miller said she had not seen you."

"No, I was down in the barn when she came up the pathway. I saw her, but she didn't see me," he replied as he went to the sink to wash his hands.

After cleaning up, Joe walked over to look at the table and said, "I don't see any food."

Mrs. Miller quickly told him, "She didn't want me to put it all on the table but brought her plate over here to fill up so it would stay hot for everyone else. Give me a minute. I'll get it all over there."

"Oh no, Mandie had a good idea," Joe said, picking up a plate and going to the stove. "Just give me some of everything."

Joe filled his plate, took it back to the table, and sat down.

The two had just finished eating when they heard a horse's hooves and wagon wheels in the yard. Joe went to look out the window.

"My father has come home," he said as he sat back down to finish his coffee.

When Dr. Woodard came in the back door a few minutes later, he didn't even stop as he rushed through the room toward the hall door.

"Good morning," he said as he passed the table. "I've been around measles and I have to clean up good before I can eat. I'll see y'all later."

"That sounds bad," Joe remarked as he drank his coffee.

"Yes, it does. So you were right! Gretchen does have the measles," Mandie said.

Joe changed the subject as he asked, "And is the metal box still in your room? Or did it walk off during the night?" he teased.

"It's still there. I checked to be sure," Mandie said, hurriedly setting down her coffee cup. "I'm so glad I came home with y'all when you told me no one seemed to be living in my father's house. And just think," she added with a big smile, "I don't have to marry you now!"

"Mandie!" Joe yelled as he threw down his napkin and stood up. "Were you going to marry me when we grow up *just* because I said I would get your father's house back for you? Was there no other reason? Like love? You did tell me you loved me. Was all this a plot to have me get your father's house back for you and then you change your mind about marrying me?"

Mandie got to her feet. She was so angry she

couldn't see straight. "Joe Woodard! You are a fi-
nagling so-and-so! Were you going to get the house
back to *buy* my hand in marriage? Is that the only
reason you were going to do it? Just to force me to
keep my promise to marry you?"

Joe started yelling at the same time. "You don't
keep your promises, Mandie! I can't depend on
anything you say!"

At that moment the two were suddenly aware of
a powerful voice booming across the room.

"I will not tolerate such behavior from either of
you!" Dr. Woodard had come into the room just in
time to hear the angry words between the two
young people. "And I will not accept anything less
than an apology. You are both too old to throw tem-
per tantrums like this."

Mandie and Joe both looked at the man standing with his hands on his hips and his feet planted
firmly on the floor. Mandie had never seen Dr.
Woodard angry before, and now she almost shook
in his presence.

"I apologize, Dr. Woodard, for acting like this in
your house," Mandie said in a quavery voice. "I'm
sorry." She looked down at the floor and her eyes
flooded with tears. She angrily fought them back.

"Please forgive me, Dad," Joe said. "It's just
that—I guess you'd say my future just went up in
smoke. I'm sorry."

Dr. Woodard came across the room to the table,
pulled out a chair, and sat down. Mrs. Miller, who
had heard the whole thing, came running with food
to put on the table for the doctor. She grabbed the
coffeepot and filled his cup. He waited until she was
finished and then he spoke.

"Now your mother told me about what happened yesterday," Dr. Woodard began as he sipped his coffee and carefully watched the two young people. "Maybe I should go see Irene. Do y'all think she needs a doctor?" He looked from one to the other.

Mandie was quicker to respond, "Oh yes, Dr. Woodard, she does. She seemed to be completely passed out, and Nimrod has her in his house and wouldn't let us see her. He'd probably let you in."

"I agree," Joe added. "It wouldn't hurt to look at her."

"Then I'll run over there after I eat," Dr. Woodard said as he cut the ham on his plate. "And your mother tells me you found Samantha, and I thank the good Lord for that."

"Yes, sir, I put her in with her puppies this morning and she seems fine," Joe said.

"And you don't know how Samantha got into Nimrod's storm cellar, is that right?" he asked as he continued eating.

"No, sir, I was so glad to find her, all I could think of was getting her home," Joe said. Glancing at Mandie he added, "Besides, Mandie talked me out of confronting Nimrod about it."

"Well then, I will take you with me, and we'll have a talk with Nimrod," Dr. Woodard said. "And I suppose I'd better stop by Miss Abigail's and get the key to the schoolhouse. Your mother told me she has had it all this time."

"Yes, sir, she has had it," Joe agreed.

Mandie remained silent because Dr. Woodard seemed to be directing the conversation to Joe. That was fine with her. She had not fully recovered from the angry words between her and Joe.

"And, Miss Amanda, what are you planning to

do with your father's house now that you own it?"
Dr. Woodard asked, looking directly at her. "You
know if you let it stand empty it will probably be
vandalized and will more or less rot away without
upkeep."

Mandie had not thought about things like that.
She frowned as she replied, "I just don't know, Dr.
Woodard. I haven't figured it all out yet."

Joe added, "And Nimrod has already told her he
would more or less cause trouble over her owning
the house. I suppose he thinks Irene should have it.
But the will states Mandie inherits the house and all
other property her father may have owned."

Dr. Woodard looked at Mandie again and said, "I
might have a solution for you. I'll let you know about
it later." He glanced across the room at Mrs. Miller
and asked, "Any more coffee?"

Mrs. Miller quickly grabbed the pot from the
stove and came rushing to refill his cup.

"Is that daughter of yours still going to marry
that fellow up at the top of the mountain?" Dr.
Woodard asked.

Mrs. Miller quickly turned back and smiled as
she said, "Yes, sir, she is. And I'll be right proud to
have him for a son-in-law." She walked back across
the room to the stove and put down the coffeepot.

Dr. Woodard quickly finished his coffee and
stood up. "All right, are you ready to go now?" he
asked Joe. "I have several other stops to make on
the way to Nimrod's, and we need to catch Mr. Tallant and give him an explanation about the missing
key. So we need to get started. We can't be late getting back."

"Yes, sir," Joe said, rising from his seat as Mandie stood up. Quickly stepping around the table,

Joe extended his hand to Mandie and said, "I apologize, Mandie, I'm awfully sorry."

Mandie quickly took his hand in hers and said, "I am too, Joe."

Joe looked at her and followed his father out the back door without another word. Mandie glanced around the kitchen. Evidently Mrs. Woodard was still sleeping or was not feeling well, because she had not come down for breakfast. Mrs. Miller was finishing up her work in the kitchen and preparing to go home.

"Could I do something to help?" Mandie offered as the woman carried dirty dishes to the sink and food back to the warmer on the stove.

"No, dear," she replied. "I'll be back later and wash these dishes, after Mrs. Woodard has her meal."

When Mrs. Miller left, Mandie decided to go down to the barn to see the puppies. She watched them scramble around in their pen, tumbling over each other, with Samantha whimpering to them now and then from where she lay in the corner. Samantha looked up when Mandie spoke to her, but she only wagged her tail and did not get up. She seemed content being back with her family.

Mandie went back inside and fastened Snowball to his leash. Then she took him outside and walked around the yard.

She didn't really have anything to do, so time seemed to drag. And she kept thinking about her outburst with Joe. She regretted that with all her heart and knew it would stay on her mind for a long time.

Finally settling down in a swing under the trees, Mandie picked up Snowball and held him in her lap as she pushed the swing back and forth. Soon she dropped off to sleep.

Before she knew it, she heard someone whistling. She rubbed her eyes and sat up to see who it was. There in the driveway was her grandmother's rig and Uncle Ned just stepping down from it. He whistled again with a big smile.

Mandie ran to him and embraced the old Cherokee, her father's dearest friend.

"Oh, Uncle Ned, I'm so glad to see you!" she exclaimed, tears of joy starting in her eyes.

Uncle Ned hugged her and then led the way to the swing where she had been sitting.

"We sit, Papoose," he told her.

Mandie sensed something was wrong, and she looked up into his troubled face.

"What is it, Uncle Ned? What's wrong? Something is wrong, isn't it?" she quickly asked.

Uncle Ned squeezed her hand and acted as though he didn't know how to answer.

"That's my grandmother's rig, I know," Mandie said. "Did she send you after me? Is she sick or something? I knew you were coming this weekend, but I thought you'd be in your wagon to take me back to school." She leaned back to look into his face.

Mandie thought she could see a tear in the old man's eyes as he finally spoke. "Sad news, Papoose. Grandmother send for Papoose. Dear President McKinley died, two-fifteen this morning." His voice trembled.

Tears poured down Mandie's face. "Oh no, Uncle Ned! The last I heard he was getting better after that man shot him. He was our friend."

"Yes, Papoose, but Big God want him to come

home," Uncle Ned continued. "Now we go to Grandmother's house."

Mandie could hardly talk. She was overcome with grief. She, Uncle Ned, her grandmother, Joe, and Uncle Ned's granddaughter Sallie had all visited the President after receiving a special invitation to his second inauguration. She had been so grateful for his friendship. And now he was gone—gone!—and wouldn't be back.

Uncle Ned held her tight until her tears finally stopped. She thought about her argument with Joe. What if *he* had died suddenly after that terrible scene in the kitchen this morning? She told Uncle Ned about it.

"I was so mean and I know I hurt Joe. I said I was sorry, but I wish I could take the mean words back," Mandie said, drying her reddened eyes.

"Always Papoose must think before doing. Think first," Uncle Ned told her. "I tell Papoose, but Papoose does not always think. Must ask Big God to forgive."

"I know," Mandie said, and looking at the clear blue sky above she said, "Dear God, please forgive me. I've been mean and hurt Joe. I'm sorry. Really sorry. Please help me to be better. Thank you, dear God. Thank you." She looked at Uncle Ned, who was smiling with his eyes closed. Evidently he had also been speaking a prayer, a silent one, to God.

At that time Mandie saw Dr. Woodard's buggy coming down the driveway. Joe was back. She watched as the doctor pulled up beside her grandmother's rig and then he stepped down and came over to them. Joe got out on the other side and didn't even glance in their direction before starting for the back door.

"Joe!" Mandie called as she ran to stop him. She grabbed his hand and said, "Joe, I'm truly sorry for what I said this morning. And I do love you. I always have—not just because of the house. I loved you before my father ever died. I know that now. Please forgive me." She gave his hand a squeeze.

Joe looked down at her and said, "I have always loved you, Mandie." He quickly put his arms around her and squeezed her tight. "Please forgive me. I was really mean this morning. I don't know what came over me except that I'm always afraid you'll meet up with someone who will take you away from me. Will you still marry me when we grow up?"

Mandie leaned back to look into his brown eyes. "My answer is still the same, Joe. When we get old enough to marry, I'll decide then."

"That's a good enough answer for now," Joe said, smiling down at her.

Mandie suddenly remembered Uncle Ned's bad news. She pulled away from Joe and said, "Uncle Ned has come to take me home. My grandmother sent for me because President McKinley has died." Her voice cracked.

Joe's face turned sad. "Oh no, I thought he was better," he said.

"So did I, but Uncle Ned said it happened at two-fifteen this morning," Mandie said.

Then Joe quickly moved away from her and said, "We didn't talk to Nimrod about Samatha, Mandie, because my father says Irene has the measles—bad. And it's highly contagious, so you and I might come down with them."

"Oh no!" Mandie said with a sudden breath. "Will Irene recover?"

"He doesn't know yet. Evidently she's had them for some time. She was alone and sick there in your father's house before we found her," Joe explained. "Oh, and he said your father's house will have to be fumigated before anyone goes back in there."

"Fumigated?" Mandie asked.

"Yes, you know, with some kind of smoke that kills germs," Joe tried to explain.

"But it has already been smoked out with all that fire," Mandie said.

"I know, and he is hoping that killed the germs so we don't catch it," Joe said.

"I don't feel too worried about that, Joe," Mandie said. "But I am worried about Irene. I sure hope she survives.

"And," Joe continued, "Dad talked to Mr. Tallant. We have his apologies."

Mandie had President McKinley on her mind now and only said, "I'm glad."

"Papoose, go," Uncle Ned called from across the yard where Dr. Woodard was talking to him. "Must go now."

The two men walked over to join Joe and Mandie.

"Dad, President McKinley is dead," Joe said.

"Yes, Uncle Ned just told me. I sure am sad about that. He was a fine, upstanding man," Dr. Woodard said.

"Home, Papoose," Uncle Ned said again.

"I'm sorry you have to go today. I was hoping you'd stay until tomorrow," Joe said.

"But my grandmother sent for me," Mandie said. Then looking up at Uncle Ned she asked, "Maybe she is planning to go to President McKinley's funeral?"

"Not know, Papoose," the old man said. "Must hurry, she said."

Mandie picked up Snowball and handed him to Uncle Ned. "Would you please hold on to him while I get my things? You know how he likes to run off."

"I hold, now hurry," Uncle Ned said as he took the cat.

Mandie got her things, met up with Mrs. Woodard in the hallway, told her goodbye, and came back outside where the others were waiting.

She smiled at Joe as Uncle Ned pulled the rig back up the driveway. As she waved, Joe called to her, "Remember what you said."

"I will," she called back.

She was going back to Asheville, where her grandmother lived. Would she be going to the President's funeral?

And of all things, Mandie was hoping she and Joe wouldn't come down with the measles. That would not only keep her out of too much school, it was also dangerous.

She had the metal box at her feet to remind her that she now owned her father's house. Uncle John would go through the legal papers for her when she got home. The house was all hers now and she wouldn't have to marry Joe just to get it back.

She thought about that as they rode along. She wouldn't have to marry Joe to get the house back, but she would marry Joe for love if she decided she loved him enough when they grew up—but that was a long way off.